A LESSER DEPENDENCY

ALMA BOOKS LTD
London House
243–253 Lower Mortlake Road
Richmond
Surrey TW9 2LL
United Kingdom
www.almabooks.com

First published by Macmillan London Limited in 1989
This edition published by Alma Books Limited in 2012
Copyright © Peter Benson, 1989

Peter Benson asserts his moral right to be identified as the author of
this work in accordance with the Copyright, Designs and Patents Act
1988

Printed in Great Britain

Typeset by Tetragon

ISBN: 978-1-84688-192-3

A LESSER
DEPENDENCY

PETER BENSON

ALMA BOOKS

'(The Ilois), mostly men and women born and brought up in the islands... live their lives in surroundings of wonderful natural beauty and in conditions most tranquil and benign.'

From a British Colonial Office Film, 1950

'The nature of (Diego Garcia) itself, which is a rather small piece of land, is also fortuitous in that it has no local population whatsoever...'

From evidence presented to US Congress Sub-Committee, March 1974

'This is the deed of me... and the adult members of my family... I am an Ilois who left that part of the BIOT never to return... we accept the money already paid... and we abandon all our claims and rights (if any) of whatever nature to return to the BIOT'

Extract from a 'Deed of Acceptance &
Power of Attorney' prepared by the
British Government in 1979

'If you liked Vietnam, you'll love Diego Garcia.'

Congressman Robert Leggett addressing the
American Congress, 1974

'There are very, very few secrets in Government.'

Tony Benn speaking to the UK Parliament's
Public Administration Select Committee on
16 March 2006. Tony Benn was a member
of the Labour cabinet that secretly agreed to
remove forcibly the Ilois from Diego Garcia
and lease the island to the USA in exchange
for a $14 million discount in the cost of
purchasing Polaris ballistic missiles.

1

In 1964, when Leonard was ten, old enough to think he knew what to expect, and bored, he walked from his home on Diego Garcia to play in a pair of wrecked planes that lay in the jungle beyond the village; operated by the British to protect their Indian Ocean interests, abandoned at the end of the second world war and haunted by the phantom buzz of bust radios and the noise of ripped wires twitching in the wind; Leonard was warned by his sister, Odette: half his age but she stared him in the eyes and shook her head.

'I'm going, anyway,' he said, and walked away from her. She watched the back of his head. He didn't turn round. 'Alright,' she said and followed him.

The sun boiled the sweat on their faces as they left their village and walked down the track that ran behind huts and vegetable gardens. Birds cried, they disturbed flocks of chickens and gangs of rats as a breeze clacked the leaves of the coconut palms that rose above the shore.

'Come on!' yelled Leonard. His sister was lingering by flowers. 'We can pick them on the way home.'

'I don't want to pick them, anyway,' she said, and caught up. 'They'd only have got in the way. They smelt nice, though,' she said, but he didn't answer.

They walked through the plantations and jungle. Coconut harvesters yelled and asked them what was happening, an abandoned animal shelter confirmed their path. Its thatch had been blown away, the roof beams were cracked and where animals had been safe was now open and pointless to mend. Whoever had built the place had given up and gone somewhere else.

An hour's walking made them hungry. Leonard said, 'I'll climb,' at a coconut tree, but Odette said, 'No. You catch.'

'Why?'

'I stretch further,' she said, and was shinning before her brother could stop her.

She climbed like a monkey, reached the nuts, waved and scared a cloud of birds away from the tree tops to the lagoon, where they flew around.

She cut a coconut and threw it to her brother. He shook his head, but he was used to her. He cracked the nut on a rock, spilt the milk and cut some flesh with a knife (his own property).

On Diego Garcia, the ocean was never more than yards away. They walked to a beach, sat on a rock, chewed and stared at familiar things. Leonard cleaned his knife on a cloth and spat into the lagoon. 'One of thee finest natural harbours in the world' – he didn't know that. Others did, though – some people who ate coconuts with forks and did polite things with napkins.

Leonard and Odette had never seen a napkin. They wiped their mouths with the backs of their hands and watched the sea rustle the coral flakes and leave tiny shells in ridges by their feet. The water was smooth and shone with a luminescence though the sun was high and dazed them. Tiny fish came to the shallows and dipped around, watching for food. The boy tossed some coconut into the water. The pieces sank, the fish sucked and blew.

'We should have a net.'

'They're not worth it.'

'Nice colours, though. See...'

Beach disappeared over every horizon, thick and constantly moving jungle fringed the frame. A stand of palm trees whispering, wild donkeys butting each other in clearings, the distant rumble of the coconut train and the call of a fisherman in the lagoon. He was casting into deep water, seeing the fish before they knew he was about.

'That's Christian's father,' said Leonard.

'No. It's Michel.'

'It isn't...'

'Leonard! I know who it is!'

'You...'

'MICHEL!' yelled Odette.

'YES!'

They could have stayed on the beach for hours, but the thought of the forbidden made Leonard stand up and say, 'Come on!' He tucked his knife into his belt.

They walked for the rest of the morning and half the afternoon before reaching the planes. Odette had been saying they were lost and should have done something else when Leonard brushed away some undergrowth and saw them.

'NO!' he yelled, 'LOOK!'

The planes were Catalina flying boats, blown from their marine moorings by rare cyclonic winds in 1944. Twenty years of jungle growth had swamped them, but in places their hulls shone through the vegetation. Leonard's eyes widened as he moved towards them. Odette shook her head. She wasn't impressed by other people's junk.

'I'll be swimming,' she said.

'Don't go far,' he said.

She smiled. 'You're scared!'

'Me?' He looked at her. 'Scared?'

'You are. You've got that look on your face. I can tell. I always know.'

'You can't. Don't pretend you're Mother.'

Odette looked away. 'I'm going swimming.'

Leonard sat in the remains of one of the aeroplanes and hummed to himself. He tried to imagine it breaking from the jungle and rising to circle the lagoon before dipping and flying west.

West (1200 miles away) was Mauritius – his father had been there – it was a big country. He climbed into the place where the cockpit had been, sat down beneath a faded pin-up of Dorothy Lamour and imagined the smashed instruments and broken controls working and clouds passing.

He thought about other countries he could be flying over, and oceans, as the noise of Odette's swimming came through the trees. Africa, France, England.

He was thinking when something cracked in the jungle and everything hushed. Birds stopped singing, and when he listened for his sister, her splashing seemed to melt away. Another crack, a breeze and the sun was sinking.

Stories of spirit pilots and the phantom buzz of broken radios had attracted Leonard, but when he was alone and where some ghosts might be, a creeping zinged down his spine and jangled in his ankles. Crack, again, and he yelled 'oi!', jumped out of the 'plane and ran through the jungle to the beach.

'What?'

'I heard something! By the 'plane.'

'Of course you did. All sorts of things live out here,' she said, and walked out of the water and along the sand.

'But it wasn't just anything. It was breathing.'

'You couldn't hear that!'

'I could!'

'Scared now?' said Odette.

'No... I'm not.'

They walked home as the sunset took daylight and wrung it bloody red. Pieces of sky turned fleshy pink and burnt into the night, boiling the sea orange, turning it gold where it met the sun...

'We'll be late for food,' said Odette, and pulled her brother along the beach.

'It'll keep.'

'Not hot. You want it hot?'

'Alright.'

Leonard's imagined crack followed him through the trees. He wondered what shape and colour it was. He had heard all about the spirits Georges' mother worried about. Odette mumbled about why did she always end up following him.

They passed a hamlet. People called and gutted fish on stones. Other children played with ducks, women didn't bother to worry. Cats chased rats up trees. The smell of cooking and woodsmoke, and the cry of a bird drifted across the lagoon as the roar of surf broke along the seaward reefs.

'Come on,' said Odette. 'We've walking to do…'

'I am!'

'Faster.'

'I can't.'

They walked as the stars came out and the lights of their village blinked across the water. These illuminated the old huts and neatly thatched roofs. A signpost pointed to places everyone knew the direction to; old people whispered. Three men pushed a stalled jeep along the road as Leonard and Odette walked up the beach and were home to their mother's 'I was going to call you. It's hot!'

2

East Point, Diego Garcia's largest village, had a shop where the islanders – the Ilois – could stock up. It could supply food, clothes, fishing tackle, wine and wedding rings (sold on the understanding that a Christian wedding was planned). Its counter was worn and marked from people's hands rubbing it and knives, sometimes. The shopkeeper was a whittler. He was whittling when Leonard appeared, kicked a stone and asked for a barrel or crate.

'Take a crate. I've got plenty. They'll only go on the fire.' He pointed to some.

'Thank you.'

'Thank you for asking. You could have had it anyway, but it was better having you ask.'

'Odette told me to.'

'She's a good girl. She was here yesterday and I thought that. For such a young girl too – full of news.' The shopkeeper shook his head at the thought.

'She looks after me.'

Leonard dragged the crate home, sat on the beach and watched his father in his boat on the lagoon. A flock of birds soared over it, waiting for scraps as coconut and banana trees waved in a lazed, generous breeze. A crab scuttled across the beach. The sky was clear and deep blue. The sun rose.

Leonard pulled the crate down to the tide-line and yelled to his sister.

'What?'

'Come here. Help me,' he said.

'What?' Odette didn't hear on purpose. She wanted to clean a duck. She had reared it herself.

'Help me!'

'I'm cleaning the duck…'

'But I can't move this!' The crate had snagged on some rocks. He tugged. 'It's stuck.'

The sea was as clear as breath. A lorry back-fired and stalled on the road behind them. Their father cast a line, squinted at something he couldn't make out on the shore, and he waited.

Ducks had been introduced to Diego Garcia by enterprising people with good ideas. Aylesburys, Khaki Campbells… Odette's was a Muscovy. The breed is a good forager, intelligent, grows quickly to an enormous size, and though not a heavy layer the female is an attentive sitter. They are not averse to life in the tropics – Piebald, Plain White, Black and Blue, Black and White – the breed comes in a range of colours, all have yellow legs.

They have a reputation for bad-tempered behaviour, and many breeders treat them as geese or keep Cayugas instead, but Odette knew nothing about this. Hers was gentle, let her stroke his bill, and didn't think for a moment that his mistress was anything but sentimental about him. He didn't know he was meat. He couldn't count to five, he didn't know she'd forget his noise. She smiled and kissed the top of his head.

'It's stuck!' Leonard would not give up. He heaved and fell over. Odette said, 'Leonard,' to the duck, and shook her head.

'Please!'

'I'm coming,' she said, and went to help.

He pulled and she pushed until the crate bounced off the rocks and into the lagoon. He picked up a paddle and steered out. She gave one last push. She stood up to her waist in the water and her dress floated around her like a flower-bed. Leonard balanced himself, sat back and headed for his father.

'I'm coming!'

'Don't sink!' Odette yelled. 'I'm not saving you!'

'I don't need saving!'

'Good. Because I won't.'

'I wouldn't want you to, even if I was!'

No wind.

The sound of splashing and barely moving ocean-swept miles. It touched a sand spit and dabbed at some beach grass. The sun boiled, sheets of heat slammed anything that moved.

Nothing moved. A veil came down and covered everything, so any noise became silence, silence curled like smoke and turned into a sound. A coconut dropped out of a tree, thudded onto the beach, rolled across a line of weed and into the sea. Odette blinked and broke the spell. She watched her brother paddle away, whistling and waving his free hand above his head.

Raphael watched his son come in a crate. He shook his head and reeled his line. He looked at his catch and gobbed a ball of phlegm into the air. He tidied a corner of sail and leant over the side.

'What're you doing out here!' he shouted. A reminding puff of wind blew off the ocean and ruffled the lagoon. 'And in that! You could drown!'

'It's not leaking! I could go further than you...'

'But you won't.'

'Why not?'

'Because you stop here.' Raphael tossed a rope. 'And catch that.'

The rope was long and heavy. Raphael had brought it years before and coiled it carefully. 'Pull yourself in,' he said, and he hauled the sail before picking Leonard out of the crate and sitting him in the boat.

'I paddled all that way,'

'You're a big boy now.'

Raphael had done the same when he was a boy. He tied the crate to the back of the boat and let Leonard steer home. 'Once,' he said, 'I steered for my father to a ship that moored... there.' He pointed across the lagoon to where the remains of a jetty stuck out. 'We gave them vegetables and chickens for their beer and cigarettes. I had a photograph taken.'

'A photograph? Where?'

'I never got it. He was going to post it but forgot. I kept a cigarette packet but it blew off.'

'What did you keep it for?'

'It had a woman on it, sitting on a gate in America. There was a mill and an aeroplane.'

'I could look for it.'

'No point.' Raphael shook his head, stood up and began to furl the sail. 'I lost it years ago.'

An hour later, Odette's duck ruffled its feathers and aimed a beady eye at Raphael. The man flashed a knife. It was sharp, likely and its tip was serrated. 'Here.'

'Now?'

'Hold him,' he said to Leonard.

A pair of dogs barked at a lorry. The humidity was steady. The duck quacked.

Leonard laid the duck on its back and put a stick across its neck. The sound of laughter drifted across the lagoon.

Odette smiled. Her friend was going to be a meal, stuffed and roasted, surrounded by cooked vegetables on a table set up on the beach. She fetched a chair.

Her mother was sorting rice. She had a jar of coconut milk to pour over the bird and a pile of tomatoes.

'Maude?' Raphael called her. 'Fetch a sack. I'll do it now.'

'I've got this one.'

'It'll do.'

Everyone was happy; they looked forward to eating and watched Raphael strop the knife before taking the duck's beak, pulling it and snapping the neck. He cut the head off, tossed it onto the beach and started to pluck. Feathers filled the air, Odette sneezed, a dog picked up the head and took it away.

Leonard stuffed the bag with feathers while the knife dripped on the beach. Maude told him to wash it off before she poured some drink and sat down to wait for the duck to cook.

3

A tractor hauling guano stalled and spilt half its load on the road behind Maude's hut. The driver shrugged, said, 'Suppose I've got to fetch a shovel,' and began to walk back the way he'd come. Maude watched him go before shouting, 'Fetch some bags! And buckets! Quickly.' She pointed at the guano. 'We'll have some of that, RUN!'

Many people collected the guano and carried it home for their gardens. Leonard threw some at Odette. When he showed Maude, the woman didn't say anything. She was carrying a wild donkey. She was small, but the donkeys were small too, more like big dogs.

She was digging the garden and waiting for guano. She heard a donkey in a ditch, so she climbed into the ditch and began to heave the animal out. Leonard and Odette came back to find her walking out of the jungle with it in her arms, and when they asked her what she was doing she said, 'Giving it a lift.'

The children laughed and said something stupid, but they couldn't see their mother's expression. The donkey was in the way. Small donkey, small face, a big laugh for the children. But the animal had broken a leg and couldn't walk on its own. It struggled but Maude could restrain it. A rooster crowed.

'He's broken his leg,' said Maude.

'Will it mend?' said Odette.

'In the end. He'll need tending.'

'I'll help.'

'I know you will.'

'Me too,' said Leonard. He was quieter than his sister, and often left out. Not this time – he arranged some leaves under a propped sheet of galvanised. 'He'll like this bed,' he said.

'It's better than ours!'

'Or mine!' Maude laughed and pinched him, and when the tractor driver arrived with a shovel she laughed as the man scratched his head and stared at the sky, as if the guano had been sucked up and into the clouds.

Like her children, her parents and her grandparents' grandparents whose bodies had been mourned with the spirit-seeker and the story-teller present at Minni-Minni, Maude had been born on the island, dropped in the sand and tuned to the rhythms of tiny island life or twisted like a lemon in a drink. Doing the same things for years. She felt messages in her bones.

Presentiment. She felt a spasm, just sitting on the veranda. A girl had gone into labour, three miles away. No relation, it was evening, Maude ran all the way without telling anyone where she was going. Leonard and Odette watched her go and sat down to wait for their father to come home.

The girl was lying on coconut mats with women all around. The atmosphere in the hut was warm and relaxed; a chicken sat on the bed and blinked.

Maude acted as reassurer to the girl, who trusted the woman. Maude's reputation had aged to myth; the best counsellor, confessor and soother. A dog barked, some men hung about outside with bottles, back early from the plantations and wanting food now; they drank, smoked cigarettes and listened for the girl to take long, deep breaths.

She did. The sun bent flowers out of clouds and the girl went 'woo woo woo'. 'Woo woo woo!' Maude held her hand and made her count 'One, two three, four... count sparrows in the trees!' she said, and patted a damp cloth across the girl's forehead.

When the contractions quietened and the girl rested her head to one side and gazed at the lagoon through gaps in the walls, Maude dampened her own forehead and remembered her children coming. They had been easy births, and both times Raphael had helped. He was an unusual Ilois man, and took time off from work in the plantations to be there. His big hands were cut but gentle when they wrapped themselves around one of hers and he told her to count. 'Count sparrows in the trees,' he'd said, 'or wagons on the coconut train.' It had been trundling through the jungle as Leonard's head appeared and when Raphael yelled about 'a boy!' Maude sat up immediately, took the child, wiped his face and said, 'Pass me a cloth. Just look at the mess! I can't do it with my hands...'

She was shaken out of her memories when the girl moaned from her belly and let the sound build through her body to a yell that shocked the chicken off the bed, out of the door and into the sunlight.

'Steady,' said Maude.

The midwife said, 'It's coming now; don't push... push... wait...' Maude said, 'Listen to her,' when the girl shook her head. 'Do as she says.'

The baby was born as Leonard and Odette, bored at home and curious to know what their mother was doing, came and stood by the door to watch.

'He looks like a fish,' said Leonard.

'He's a girl, fool,' said Odette, and 'it's only because she's slimy.' She shook her head. Her brother related everything to fishing, and didn't stay long enough for anyone to ask what he was doing there. He went and sat on the beach to count boats as they tacked across the lagoon; the evening was cool. When Maude was thanked, she said, 'Fetch him,' to Odette, and the three walked home as the sky ripened like a fruit and spat last pips of light into the night.

Raphael was waiting for them at home. He had been in the plantations late and, tired, stretched across the veranda to doze. Work had been hard... he wished he could fish all day. Generations of Ilois had bred absolute knowledge of the lagoons and waters around the island; every reef and headland was traced into his genes. The strength of the currents there, the depth of water here. He was thinking, as he dozed, about a reef in the north, beyond Simpson Point.

Maude tapped him in the side with her foot and said, 'Elaine had a little girl.'

He opened his eyes. 'It wouldn't have been a big one…'

'It could have been. Look at the boy.' Maude pointed at Leonard. 'He was big; long. Remember?'

Raphael thought about that. 'I suppose so,' he said, and went to fetch a bottle his friend Georges had given him.

Georges was a massive man with massive biceps and a broken nose. He could split a coconut with a light tap, and stare birds to death. He lived with his mother. She was old and mumbled about spirits from Madagascar, but was happy when she was sat in a chair with a whisk to keep flies off and a piece of string. She'd fiddle with the string and let Georges drink at crossroads or passing places along the tracks.

'We should ask him to eat,' said Raphael. 'And his mother. She never gets out.'

'She doesn't eat.'

'She must!'

'Raw eggs. That's all.'

'She could come anyway. Georges can carry the chair over. She'd like the change. All she ever does is sit and stare at the same thing every day.'

'She's old.'

'I know that.'

'Good. Then catch something different. There's ripe aubergines; we'll eat something special.'

Raphael laughed. 'Different? What you mean? I catch different every day!'

'I know,' she said, and touched his knee.

Georges came to eat on a Saturday. He carried his mother over and then her chair, and set her up on Maude's veranda. She was amazed to see the lagoon from a different angle, and complained that spirits had come and were spreading salt in everyone's eyes, when everyone knew spirits avoided salt. They were deceiving them before something happened.

'Nothing's going to happen, Mother,' said Georges. 'Look; here's eggs, and in a bowl. You don't normally get a bowl, do you?'

'No.'

'It makes a change, doesn't it?'

She didn't like a change. She shook her head, ate the eggs and dropped the bowl. He stuck his broken nose close to her face and smiled. He had three teeth and patted her head. If anyone hurt her he would strangle them.

He said, 'I'll be over there,' and pointed to a fire on the beach. 'I'll watch you.'

'Good.'

He had brought a bottle of calou, a dangerous drink made from the sap of coconut trees; he poured cups and played with Leonard and Odette. He let them hit him but they couldn't hurt him. They punched his chest, his legs and his arms but he just roared with laughter and wouldn't fall over. He picked them up and tossed them into the lagoon.

'There!' he shouted. 'That's what I do to children.' They laughed. He let them have a sip of calou.

Maude cooked aubergines in a sauce of coconut juice, onion, chillies and tomatoes, and served them with lobsters. Georges told a story about a broken tractor, Raphael threw a rock at a rat, and after the food had been eaten and the children put to bed, the adults lay on the beach, poked the cooking fire and drank. The moon rose and veined the lagoon with phantom, still light.

Georges' mother grunted.

'I'll fetch some more,' Georges said, went to his hut and came back with two bottles of wine. 'You'll like this,' he said. 'It's fresh.'

'Fill mine,' said Raphael.

'Women first. Maude?'

'Go on.'

Georges drank fast, lit a cigarette and slurred, 'You know... I have a secret.'

'What's that?'

Georges looked at his mother. She was asleep but he whispered when he said, 'Something no one else knows. Only her and me. We kept it from everyone.'

'Did you?'

'So if I tell you, you've got to promise not to tell anyone. It's very...'

'Promise,' said Raphael.

'And me,' said Maude.

'Good,' Georges whispered. He belched and swayed in his seat. 'Good. Then I'll tell you...'

'What?'

He lowered his head and mouthed the words first before saying, 'I'm a German,' and drinking some more wine.

Maude laughed. Georges looked at her. Her eyes reflected the moonlight on the ocean, and when she brushed a fly away he felt an unusual quiver in his stomach.

'What's funny?'

'Nothing. It's just that you're...'

'German. At least half.' And he amazed Raphael and Maude with a story that was a lie. They knew it, but he'd told it to himself so many times that he didn't doubt a word of it. He spilt some drink and said, 'But don't tell anyone.'

'You said that.'

Georges claimed that his father had been a sailor on a German warship that visited Diego Garcia 'a long time ago'. Raphael didn't laugh. It was true about the warship. Sailors had come ashore and mended some Ilois boats, but everyone knew Georges' father had gone to Peros Banhos and not come back. Georges trying to convince people with stories didn't do him any good.

'German,' said Maude, when he'd finished. 'Maybe I should tell you a secret.'

Raphael sat up. He didn't know his wife had secrets.

'What is it?' said Georges.

'Me and him are British.'

'But not real Britons,' said Georges. 'There's real German blood in here.' He tapped his arm. 'Pints.'

'Yes!' said Maude and she reminded him about the doctors, teachers, policemen and administrators who called on the island. She had a paper Union Jack to wave at administrators and could yell, 'Long live the Queen!'

Raphael watched the tide and only half listened to the argument. Instead, he thought about fish he'd surprised in past nights. Night fishing was often more successful than day fishing – he turned this thought over, looked at it from all angles and stood up when Georges said, 'And you can't make oil from books…'

'I'm going fishing,' he said, and clapped. The fire died down. 'I'll take a lamp. You can help push out.'

'Me?' Georges finished a bottle and squinted.

'You can do it.'

'I don't know.' Georges had had enough to drink. He wouldn't bother to work in the morning.

'I can't do it on my own,' said Raphael, and he carried a lamp to the boat, tied it in the stern and coiled some lines into a bag.

Georges nodded. 'Right,' he said, put his shoulder to the stern of the boat and pushed.

'Harder, German!'

'It's stuck!'

'No, it's not. Nothing's ever stuck! You're not trying!'

When the boat was floating, Georges gave Raphael a shot of wine, waved him over the lagoon and watched until the stern lamp was a pin-prick. Then he walked back to the fire and sat next to Maude.

'No,' she said.

On Diego Garcia, other men sometimes took the place of absent husbands at night. Not Maude's bed. She had enough to do, and when he tried to kiss her she said 'Take her home,' and pointed to his mother. She had slumped back in her chair, and was snoring. 'Go on.'

He shrugged and said 'One day, Maude.'

'One day never!'

'We'll see,' he whispered.

She heard that but didn't say anything else. He staggered around and moaned about 'a headache now'. It was his fault. If he was always going to be stupid she would treat him like a child. 'Go home now, German,' she said, and pinned a canvas sheet across the door of her hut. 'Good night.'

4

Raphael sat in his boat in the dark with a slack line. A few late lights burned along the shore, the only buildings he could see were the copra sheds at East Point, shadowed against the palms.

They were owned by a company called Chagos Agalega: the buildings, yards, plantations beyond and the railway. Raphael and Georges' work for them involved cutting coconuts, planting young palms and clearing undergrowth with hoes and machetes (owned by the company). They were paid in food, medical expenses and a small cash sum, banked for them by the company.

As Raphael ran a finger down his line he didn't want to think about work. He envied old men who could fish all day like his father had done in the last years of his life. Too old to be useful in the jungle he had taken to the lagoon and hardly come ashore. Insisting that one day his son would overtake his footsteps and fish all day without needing to work for Chagos Agalega, he had taught the boy to swim.

Raphael had taken to the water like a bucket. He had no coordination, and it took him months to swim a yard. He couldn't tell his legs to kick without the rest of his body thinking it was time to sink. His father almost lost patience with him many times, but was a drinking man and, in the end, didn't care if his son couldn't sort himself out. But Raphael had been stubborn early, and swore at his father inside. He would prove he could swim. He practised secretly and then bet him he could swim from a jetty to some rocks.

'You've got nothing to bet with!'

'I have.' Raphael showed his father a collection of shells.

'I could pick things like that up any time. Look! There's some here.'

'But these are mine!'

Raphael's father had stared at his boy. He narrowed his eyes and farted. He took a coin out of his pocket and put it on a rock. 'That,' he said, 'against the shells. Go!'

Raphael swam the distance and bought a cake with his winnings. He carried it hidden up his shirt with his head down, and ate it all alone, in a glade outside Marianne.

Raphael was shaken out of his thoughts by a bite. Something small grabbed the bait and he took the strain. It wriggled free then, and the line went slack.

5

Two weeks later, Raphael smiled sweetly when Georges said, 'You couldn't catch a sweat!' Another fishing trip had ended in tangled lines and an empty bag.

'At least I try. All you do is nothing!'

'I've got my mother to watch!'

'Her and a bottle.' Raphael smelt his friend's breath and waved his hands. 'I know.'

Georges needed a drink at eleven in the morning to set him even. He had persuaded his boss to give him wine instead of cooking oil. He smoked too much and kept apart from most of his work-mates. They weren't involved or insulted. He scared them. His (company) machete was always kept sharp. He wrapped it in an oiled cloth each evening, and walked home slowly with a filled screw-top bottle he'd owned for five years. This fitted in his pocket and was his prize possession. It had GILBEYS written in raised letters around its neck. He topped it up twice a day.

His mother was waiting for him. She hadn't noticed him leaving in the morning, and wondered if it was him coming home. She had lost her mind in 1959, when a lorry had demolished her previous hut. She'd been cooking and smelt oil ever since the accident. The lorry had been coming at speed from Simpson Point, where it had been overloaded by a group of six irresponsible men. She had cut her hair and embarrassed Georges for months by not staying at home.

He said, 'I'm back!' and propped his machete against a bucket. He kicked a dog off the veranda and sat down. 'Mother?'

She hadn't remembered answering a question for six years. All she could remember was a man flying through

30

the windscreen of his truck, through her hut and into a stack of brooms.

Georges laughed and shook his head. For all his behaviour he wanted to look after his mother until she died. She died in the spring. He had been in the shop.

'I'll take the usual, and a bottle of that.'

'I kept one back for you. It came in yesterday.'

'I knew it would.' It was cane spirit. 'Keep another.'

The shopkeeper tapped his own head. 'Don't worry. There's plenty more.'

'Mind there is.' Georges pulled himself up and pointed a finger. His head touched the roof.

He walked home for his lunch. Other workers sat under trees in the plantation while the sun rose directly overhead and peeled the skin off rocks. Dogs lay by taps; the only things that bothered were flies. The day ripped itself open and sighed to a dead and solid halt. Even Maude gave up working in her garden. Her hoe had made clouds of dust that drifted across the road and settled on neighbours' washing. A jeep overheated and blew up.

Georges found his mother dead in her chair. She had a surprised expression on her face and a streak of bird shit in her hair. Georges prodded her and yelled, 'Mother!'

Maude ran to see. She couldn't understand how she'd missed realising the woman was dead. Death affected her in the strangest ways. 'She must have died when that lorry crashed,' she said, to explain herself, and helped Georges lay his mother out in the hut.

Maude stayed with the body while Georges walked back to East Point. 'My mother is dead,' he said to himself. He took out his bottle and had a drink. 'My mother is dead,' he said at a house that overlooked the green.

'You've got some money?' said a man.

'Here.'

'Wait at home. We'll come in half an hour.'

'Thank you.'

'Go on.'

31

Georges walked to the shop. The man he'd spoken to was a mourner; when the shopkeeper saw him again he said, 'Back again?'

'My mother is dead.'

'Oh, Georges. Georges...'

'I just found her. She looked like she was about to say something.'

'Oh...'

'She didn't.'

'No...'

'She's dead.'

A woman came to buy some soap but the shopkeeper waved her away. He put his hand on Georges' shoulder. 'What do you need?'

'More drink. And some tea. Coffee?'

'Here...'

'Can I pay tomorrow? I haven't got any...'

'Next week, any time.'

'Come tonight.'

'I'll bring some more.' He tapped some bottles and smiled. 'No charge.'

When Georges got home, Maude had swept the hut and left the rubbish in a pile beneath the shelf. She'd ringed it with shells and laid a clean sheet of her own over the body. The mourners came, wailed, and in the evening people came from every village on the island and remembered the corpse as a walker.

Maude knelt Odette beside her and prayed for the spirit to find itself a solid boat, warm winds and calm seas home. She fingered the shroud and when she'd finished said, 'Open a bottle for Georges.' He was sitting in a corner.

'Come on, Georges!'

A man from Balisage began a song about graves opening and spirits flying to Africa. He had a deep voice and no one joined him in the first verse. Another man sang the chorus and waited for a drum in the second verse.

Raphael passed Georges a jug as the mysterious 'spirit-seeker' stood up and began to dance. He was from Marianne, carried a switch of coconut leaves and held his eyes wide open. He looked around the crowd and whispered for the spirit to come out. He flicked at anything that moved. Children stood back. He kicked his legs, crouched down and leapt up again. The singing grew louder. Bottles were tossed into the sea. A 'story-teller' appeared and began to bother the mourners.

He pretended to be an insect and told a story about five gods and a ship that flew across the ocean with captured spirits. They laughed at people on earth – the mourners jeered. The 'spirit-seeker' waved his switch at the man and shouted. Georges covered his ears and yelled 'Mother!' over the din, but no one heard him. Maude took Odette and Leonard home, and came back with more wine. She passed the bottles around and took one to Georges.

'Here!'

When the story-teller had reached a point in his tale where the gods caught a goat, the mourners threw corks at him and chased him away. They left him on the beach and went back to play dice and cards on Georges' veranda.

The body was carried to Minni-Minni and buried there the next day. For seven nights following, a cup of tea was left out for the spirit, on the eighth a plate of unsalted food. On the ninth day, the spirit was taken away in the pile of rubbish Maude had swept under the shelf. The rubbish was carried to a distant spot by the women from the twelve huts by Georges', dumped, and in fear of the spirit of his mother haunting them no one looked back as they walked away. Ilois watched death carefully, and didn't want too much spread over so many small islands in the Indian Ocean.

'If the spirit-seeker's from Marianne, why does he have to live in a hut?' said Odette.

'There's things you don't need to know.' Maude pricked her finger on a needle. She was sewing Georges' trousers. He had

6

In 1966, Raphael sailed to Mauritius on a copra boat, the SS *Nordvaer*. The passage was slow, but the crew were friendly and told stories about women with three breasts and dogs that could stone cherries.

He had saved money in his account for two years, enough to buy all the things on the list he carried. Shirts. Material for Maude. A garden rake. A paint-brush. Rum and cane spirit for Georges. A doll for Odette and a diver's mask for Leonard.

A diver's mask would be Leonard's dream. He'd borrowed one once and the lagoon had become a place he had not dreamed existed. Swimming underwater with his eyes open, the coral reefs were transformed from the distorted shapes he'd seen from his father's boat into another world. He found mother of pearl lying like rubbish, cone shells tumbled through his wash and he met fish like family. His own mask would give him a new freedom, and a silence like the peace a hunter inspires in jungle animals. Something deep and lasting.

Ilois people often visited Mauritius for supplies they couldn't buy in the Chagos. Those who went enjoyed renewing old friendships, spending time with long lost relatives or browsing through Port Louis market for cheap goods.

Raphael stayed in Port Louis with an Ilois who had moved to Mauritius years before. Alain; working for the copra company hadn't been his line, and when Port Louis appeared to offer opportunities, he'd left Diego Garcia. But the city confused him until it beat him. A clothes shop had been beyond his means, a fruit stall too difficult to stock, a hawker's case was stolen. Saved money gone; he ended up offering a tin roof to visiting Ilois.

Tin roof, slum. It was at his place that Raphael got the first idea that something was wrong. Life snarled; he listened as he was told about stranded Ilois.

These were people Raphael knew. They'd left Diego Garcia earlier in the year and hadn't returned as expected. People on the island had been wondering where they were. Rumours had flown but ships were always getting delayed. 'But ships don't get delayed,' said Alain, 'forever! What else do people say?'

'About what?'

'About the people who haven't gone home!'

'Not much.'

'I bet.'

'Bet what?'

Dogs barked in the street outside. A woman shouted. A child cried. Alain said, 'You know they're forced to stay here.' He wagged a finger. 'They can't use their tickets…'

'Can't use them!' Raphael laughed. 'I've got one!' He showed it. He couldn't read but he knew what it meant. 'I'll use it!'

'So what?'

'So it'll get me home.'

'It won't.'

'Yes,' said Raphael, and the thought of shirts, dress material and a diver's mask blew the worries he should have had away, as he went shopping with his rupees tied to the inside of his trousers with a whipping of string.

Rupees. In the Chagos, the money banked for the plantation workers was hardly ever handled. Ilois bartered, but Raphael wasn't confused. He walked to the market. He was excited. There were more people there than lived on Diego Garcia. More people stood around one stall than lived in his village. He felt small, and shuffled around looking for the first thing on his list.

Shirts. He found some, bargained and bought, and though people jostled and recognised him as an Ilois, he didn't feel threatened. Port Louis has a warm heart, and it beats from the market, where you can buy anything and not mind what it is because you bought it there. Raphael smiled at the shirt-seller, re-tied his bundle of notes and jangled the change in his pocket.

He bought a bottle of beer from a Chinese shop, and leant against a wall. Diego Garcia's traffic and roads were nothing like the traffic and roads that knit Port Louis. He stood and watched buses trail in from Pamplemousses, Centre de Flacq, Mahebourg, Souillac, Curepipe and Beau Bassin. Lorries carrying stone and rubbish belched from building sites. Men hung from running-boards, hats off, shirts out, waving at friends and girls as they shopped and talked.

The beer was cold, and came in a brown bottle. Other people stood around with their own bottles, swigging, talking about the football pools and looking at the tourists. Some of these had big lenses, small shorts and loud shirts. They passed Raphael but didn't recognise him as British.

Port Louis baked as the sun rose, and people rushed to finish things. Cars hissed and the road-menders shaded their brooms under torn canvas sheets. Raphael finished his beer and sweated it out all the way back to his lodgings.

'Busy day?' said Alain.

'Good shirts,' said Raphael, and showed the man what he'd bought.

'How much?'

Raphael told him.

'That much?' Alain envied his guest's innocence but wouldn't sneer. He had been the same once, and remembered the time.

Raphael shrugged. 'They're worth it,' he said, and put them in his bag.

Raphael's trust and innocence shone in Mauritius. He loved streets of lights, radios with fifty switches, shirts you didn't have to wash and trousers that didn't need mending. He spent a week spending money before thanking Alain and leaving for the docks. 'The ship,' he said, 'will take me.' He smiled. 'See you next year.' The two men shook hands.

Raphael stood on the quay at Port Louis and listened as he was told there were no more sailings to the Chagos. He didn't understand. It was a mistake. He had a ticket. 'What about my wife?' he said. He showed the man the rake he'd bought her. 'My children? I've got work there. I have to go home…'

'I'm sorry,' said the man. 'There's orders.' He flashed a paper. 'We can't let you go back there.'

'It is a mistake,' said Raphael.

The man shook his head.

'What do I do then?'

The man shrugged.

Raphael promised he'd be back the next day, and with ten rupees in the world, plus a bundle of clothes, tools and a doll and a diver's mask, he walked back to Alain's, was told, 'Didn't I say so?' and spent an unplanned night on the floor.

When Alain asked him for rent there were only three rupees left and miles between him and home. He'd been planning to repaint his boat on his return to Diego Garcia. It needed it badly. He had bought a new brush for the job. He held it in his hand.

7

Maude stood on the beach and strained her powers of intuition. It was a hot day. The sun steamed the ocean, the reefs boiled and something in the air smelt.

Raphael had been gone six months. There had been no word or letter. No overseers could explain the circumstances. They shrugged and said maybe the ship needed new turbines, or maybe Raphael and a steady trickle of other missing Ilois were earning good money in Mauritius.

'There're jobs in Port Louis.'

'What jobs?'

'All sorts. Building jobs, dock work, factory work. He could be working in...'

'But he's only ever worked in plantations. That and fishing. He doesn't do that sort of work.'

'Then maybe he's fishing!'

'With his boat sitting there?' Maude pointed to his boat. It had never been idle for so long.

'Well maybe...' but the man couldn't think. He was confused, and didn't need Maude asking questions he couldn't answer. He was meant to be in authority.

'Maybe what?'

'I don't know.'

'You should.'

The overseer sniffed.

Leonard and Odette interrupted the talk. They didn't understand, and wanted feeding. Maude snapped, 'Later!' They jumped. She never snapped, raised her voice or narrowed her eyes but she began to. Raphael's absence and the absence of his income forced her. 'Later!' she said again, and sat down. The overseer coughed and left.

Georges asked to sleep on her veranda; she didn't see why not. He gave her something for the space, and she'd smack him with a pole if he bothered her. He didn't. He said she should just think about other things. 'Work,' he slurred. Working would take her mind off Raphael. One day she approached a plantation manager.

'Got a job for me?' she said. 'Anything?'

'Can you use one of these?' He showed her a knife.

'Better than you…' she said.

'Good.'

'I've got my own.'

'You can use this one.' He was a tolerant man and didn't mind the Ilois. They were some of the friendliest people he'd ever had to order about. East Point jail was hardly ever used. Life could be hard but it had never been murder. He gave Maude a job and gloves, and she started the next day.

She split coconuts and scooped the flesh out. Chagos Agalega offered her a rent-free place too, but she preferred to stay in her own. She kept Raphael's things – his rod, tackle, spare shirt – ready for him, and when she wasn't working or cooking, stood on the shore and watched the waves run empty from Mauritius.

When she worked, Leonard and Odette hung about. They played with others or chased dogs and rats away from the drying trays. More like birds than children; their laughter didn't console her. But the island didn't ring any more. The sun seemed to shine from behind clouds when there were no clouds for miles. Even Georges couldn't cheer her up. He told jokes, offered calou and said everything would be alright, but she didn't laugh, didn't drink and didn't believe him. She neglected her vegetable garden, and didn't care when the donkey went missing.

Since its leg had healed it had grown tame. It had lived in a paddock behind the hut. Maude knew it was planning to leave. Suddenly it was gone.

'Where's the donkey?' Odette said.

Maude didn't answer. She was too busy staring. She was tired, and hadn't tidied her hair for days. Georges lay on the beach and smoked a cigarette.

'Where's the donkey?' Odette asked him. 'Mother won't say. I called him.'

'Where should he be?'

'In the paddock.' She pointed. 'He comes out sometimes, but only when someone's watching. We used to feed him but I haven't seen him since yesterday.'

'You want to find him?'

'Of course,' said Odette.

Leonard nodded. He picked his nose. 'I'll help,' he said. 'I know where he'd go.'

'You don't! You never helped with him anyway. You said you would, but did you?'

'He'd go back with the wild ones.'

'He might not. They frighten him.'

Georges led the way. The children called, 'Donkey! Donkey!' but nothing answered them.

They asked people they met but everyone shook their heads. They walked as far as Minni-Minni and searched around the graves, derelict buildings and jungle that surrounded the place before giving up, sitting down and watching the sun set over the lagoon.

'He's not here,' said Georges.

'No,' said Odette.

'He'd have heard us calling,' said Leonard. 'He knew his name.'

'He never had a name! It's stupid, calling animals names. They don't speak to each other.'

'He's back with the wild ones,' said Georges.

'I told you.'

Not so many fishing boats bobbed in the lagoon as had once. The atmosphere of the place had shifted in a subtle and confusing way. Its waves didn't rise and fall with the same spirit and the shore wasn't dotted with so many lights. Some huts had

41

been abandoned and cannibalised for other places in bigger hamlets. Georges, Leonard and Odette gave up their search.

'We'll go home,' said Georges. 'The donkey's happier where he is, anyway. If he wants to come back he will. Come on.' He wanted a drink.

'That's sad,' said Odette.

Leonard nodded.

Maude was still sitting on the beach, twisting a knot of palm leaves with her fingers. She didn't care where the donkey was, and didn't answer when Georges called her name.

'Maude!'

She cooked some food. He opened a bottle. The children sat and waited, a rooster called, a neighbour arrived to tell them to be at the manager's house in the morning.

The manager of Chagos Agalega gave his workers the news. The British had bought the company and were closing it down. The factories would be closed soon, the plantations abandoned and all salvageable machinery shipped out. He watched faces as he explained the situation, and felt gentle puffs of tropical wind flap his trouser legs.

'What did he say?'

'They were orders. They're closing.'

'Do we keep our knives?'

'Bloody knives,' said Georges, and held up his thumb. He'd cut it badly. 'It hurts.'

He'd gone to visit the nurse. She had left for Mauritius and wasn't coming back. He went to the shop to buy a bandage. They didn't have any and didn't know when the next lot would come in. Supply ships had stopped sailing to the Chagos.

'I'm bleeding!'

'Georges! I had Marcel in yesterday. You've seen his leg?'

'Yes.'

'He needs more than a nurse. The man can't move. Jean carried him down but I couldn't do a thing.'

'Then give me a bottle.'

'Hardly any good ones left now, either. God knows.'

'What?'

'I don't know...' said the shopkeeper and went to his back room.

Georges walked to Maude's with the bottle. The first rain in months washed the island. Big drops forcing palms droopy, filling holes in the roads and tracks. More people cleared their shelves, deserted their homes and took ships to Mauritius. The railway tracks that had served the factories rusted, old wagons lay on their sides in deserted sidings. The plantations grew wild and women wearing nothing but vests scavenged abandoned company houses.

8

Raphael ran out of money and had to sell his shopping. He went back to a hardware store with the rake. He showed it to a Chinaman and explained his circumstances. The Chinaman didn't understand, but gave him some money for the tool. Half what he had paid in the first place, but it meant food.

Shirts, paint-brush, Odette's doll, dress material, all went the same way, until he was left with Leonard's diver's mask. He sat outside Alain's shack and held it in his hands. He looked at it, played with its strap and hoped that one day his son would be able to fish all day in the Chagos.

'What you got?'

'This.' He held it up. 'Leonard'll be wondering where it is. He'll think I've let him down.'

Alain laughed. 'You've let him down!' He spat and laughed again.

'What's funny?'

'Nothing...'

'No! What?'

'Nothing. Really. I can't say.'

No one could get any sense out of people at the docks. Raphael had given up trying to get home months before. He just thought there was something wrong with the ship. It was all he could think. Other Ilois had ideas about what was happening, but no one took any notice of them. Ilois had always been loyal to the Queen and cherished goods with 'Made in Britain' printed on them.

Raphael thought about these things as he sat on a wall overlooking the docks. Ships rode at anchor and the Customs House was busy. Lorries hauled cargoes from the warehouses and grain stores. Fork-lift trucks reversed into pallets and stacks. People shouted, turned up radios and rushed around. Hooters blared, chains rattled and a clock chimed the hours.

He put his hands over his ears. One of the worst things about Mauritius was noise. All day and every night: cars, trucks, buses, people shouting, radios. Diego Garcia had had noise but nothing like Port Louis's. He wanted the peace at home, the only sound the slap of water against the side of his boat as a fish took the bait. The swish of a line, the rush of his heart to his mouth. Something special for Maude to cook...

'Something different.'

'I always catch different! What do you mean?'

Raphael sold Leonard's diver's mask on a wet day in July. An unlikely wind had blown a belt of rain over Port Louis and sent everyone for cover. He'd been standing in the bus station, asking people if they wanted to buy a mask, and found himself sheltering between a wall and a tourist.

This tourist – a man – was wearing a bright shirt and nodded at Raphael. He rubbed his arms to indicate cold. Raphael held up the mask and rubbed his stomach. The tourist pointed to his own chest. Raphael nodded. The tourist scratched his chin and looked at Raphael. He saw a small, hunched man with a straggly beard and dull eyes. His clothes were hanging off his back, his shoes were broken. His toes poked out and twitched. He held up five fingers and pointed at the mask.

'Five?' said the tourist.

Raphael nodded.

The tourist fished in his pocket and gave Raphael five rupees. A bargain. He took the mask. He smiled, patted Raphael on the shoulder and took a taxi to Flic en Flac.

For a month of his life on Mauritius Raphael tried to help himself. Alain said fishermen always wanted mates, so he splashed water on his face and brushed his hair.

'Where?' he asked.

'Port Louis, Tombeau, Grand Baie. Ask anyone.'

Raphael asked. He had to know. The ocean, fish, a slack sail on flat water. He wanted to feel salt caked into the lines that covered his face; he asked people at Port Louis docks.

'You need a worker?' and he'd point at the sea.

'Not today, old man.'

Old man? He shook his head and said he wasn't, but no one believed him.

'Not today.'

'When?'

'I don't know...'

'I can do everything those men are doing.' He pointed across the wharf to where a gang were grappling a bale of cotton.

'Not today. Okay?'

He set out for Tombeau. He walked slowly, dodged traffic and begged water along the way. He found bananas in a tree, and though they weren't ripe he was hungry enough to steal and eat three. They sat in his stomach but he walked on until he reached the bay and the first decent shore he'd seen since leaving the Chagos.

He strolled along it, wandered into the ocean and picked up shells and seaweed. He smelt the air. It was fresh and reminding. He wanted to stay so he found a grassy place, sat beneath a tree and watched fishing boats trace erratic wakes between the shore and the reef that broke in a dangerous line beyond them.

'Hey!'

Raphael didn't look up. He had watched the boats for an hour and would watch for another.

'Hey! You!'

Tombeau Bay was a good place to be. It didn't come close to home but was closer than Port Louis. He took a deep breath, held it and closed his eyes.

'Off! Move, go on!' A man shouted at him. He was angry and yelled, 'What's the matter with you? Deaf?'

Raphael was startled. He stood up and shook his head. 'No,' he said.

'Then sit on the beach, not in my garden. I'm not a hotel for people like you.'

'Your garden?' Raphael didn't understand. On Diego Garcia, everyone's garden belonged to everyone else.

'Yes!' said the man, and pointed to a sign. 'It's private! Go on! Off!'

'But I was only...'

'OFF!' The man pointed again. Raphael stood up and shook his head as he walked away.

He walked around the bay and asked some fishermen if they needed help. 'I can work,' he said, but none of them believed him. 'I lived in the Chagos. My own boat...'

They shook their heads, coiled ropes and pointed up the coast. 'Try Grand Baie or Perybere,' they said. 'Plenty of work there. It's better fishing.'

Raphael sighed. 'How far?'

'Fifteen miles,' said one.

'Ten by the road,' said another.

'You'll make it...'

'Will I?'

'Easy.'

The morning turned into afternoon. The fishermen began to eat lunch. They offered Raphael some fish and bread. He thanked them, ate, and when they'd finished and went back to work, he watched them for ten minutes before taking the road to Grand Baie.

The air was clammy and full of exhaust fumes. Fields of sugar cane lined the roads. He passed through villages full of saried women and men outside shops talking about other men. Corrugated shacks, washing on bushes, barefoot children chasing dogs through gardens.

Adverts he couldn't read for Fanta and Coke. Buses, bicycles, more sugar cane.

Some goats. A mosque. Schoolchildren in clean clothes carrying baskets and exercise books.

A garage with a pile of bald tyres for sale, all marked

'NEW!' Men working at sewing machines in back yards. Ginger dogs.

Night fell before he reached Grand Baie, so he spent the night in a ditch beside a tobacco field outside Triolet, stole a pineapple in the morning and ate it as he walked the last few miles.

He liked Grand Baie caught in its first clip with morning. Fishing boats, tourist yachts, glass-bottoms and motor boats rode a falling tide. Some men stood on the sweep of coral sand, scratched their heads and looked at the weather.

A few clouds moved by inches as the sky billowed with warmth, and the sun rose. The smell of breakfasts cooking and coffee, blinds going up in boarding houses, curtains being drawn in some big hotels. A cow sitting in the road.

Raphael asked a dozen fishermen for work until one didn't say, 'No.' 'Why?' the man said.

'Because...' Raphael didn't know what to say. He wasn't used to questions.

'Can you clean fish?' the man said. 'I can't stop to show you. It's busy here.'

'Yes.'

'Tie lines? Bait hooks?'

Raphael nodded. 'I was in the Chagos. I had my own boat; lines and everything.'

The man scratched his head. He knew about Ilois, and though he had heard they were unreliable he believed Raphael's story. He saw black in the man's eyes, and he did need help with his boat, his catches and his tackle. His brother had been helping him, but had got work on a glass-bottom. So he said, 'Yes', shook hands with Raphael, said, 'Maurice', and Raphael said, 'Raphael'.

9

A rainstorm forced Maude, Leonard, Odette and Georges to shelter in an abandoned copra store; the noise of a dumper truck drifted across the lagoon, and chainsaws whined in the jungle. American naval construction workers (Seabees) had arrived on Diego Garcia. They yelled, palms split, rats and the rain ran in streams through the store.

'I'm hungry,' said Leonard.

'We're all hungry!' Maude snapped.

'We'll find something later,' said Odette.

'Will we?'

'Yes. We always do, don't we?'

Maude thought about that. 'No we don't. And I can't see why.'

She had lost weight and her patience. Her powers of intuition had been warped by the circumstances. When she narrowed her eyes and closed her mind to everything around her all she could see was a mist swirling around screaming people. She couldn't see their faces and didn't recognise their voices – they were familiar – but she preferred not to know who they were.

The rain gave up after an hour and Georges said, 'Let's see what they're doing.' He pointed across the lagoon to where the Seabees were working. He wanted to see their machines. Diego Garcia's tractors and lorries were old and rusting. Some of the diggers the Americans owned were yellow and shone in the sunlight. They were greased and fast across the beaches and into the jungle after all the trees. 'You coming? We'll get close to them.'

'Alright.'

He entertained the children with a song as they walked around the lagoon. They smiled, but not like they used to.

They couldn't understand why life was so different or why their mother had changed; she lagged behind and kicked stones into the sea.

The palms dripped as the clouds rolled away and left a washed, pale sky hanging across the horizon. An American supply boat rode at anchor. The sun glittered its fittings; a chainsaw stopped, a tractor hauled trunks out of the jungle and dumped them on damp fires.

Smoke filled the air. Maude and the others sat on palm stumps and watched the work. A Seabee saw them and waved them over.

'Howdy!'

The Ilois nodded.

'Bob!' The American held out his hand. The Ilois shook it. 'You wanna drink?' He smiled. 'Cigarettes?'

The Ilois shook their heads.

Bob made a motion of hand to mouth. 'Drink?' he said again.

Georges understood. 'Yes,' he said, and smiled back.

Bob went to a hut and came back with cans of beer and Coke, and bars of chocolate. Maude took one of these without a word and peeled its wrapper carefully. She folded the paper and the foil separately, tucked them in her skirt and divided the chocolate equally.

The last time any of them had tasted chocolate was so long gone it was barely memory. They ate with their eyes closed, swigged the drinks and thought, for a second, that things could change back to how they had been before. Peace, cultivated vegetable gardens, laying chickens, the copra factories working. Enough food. Maude opened her eyes and watched another palm topple into the lagoon. The fires recovered from the rainstorm and threw massive spitting flames into the air.

Bob looked at the Ilois. He didn't know anything about them. All he was doing was clearing jungle and laying concrete. Thin natives were unexpected.

'Have some more,' he said, and, 'You're hungry.'

'Cigarettes?' said Georges.

'Better than that!' He left and came back with more food. More chocolate and some other rations. Beef stew in packets, macaroni cheese in bags and a bag of oranges. 'Here,' he said, 'take it.' And he rolled a joint.

He smoked. Georges watched. 'You wanna toke?' He offered. 'Philippino,' he said.

Georges smiled. It was months since his last cigarette. He thanked Bob and took a drag. It tasted and rushed to his head. It banged his ears together, said 'Hello' and 'Goodbye' at the same time and shrunk his eyeballs to the size of peas. He coughed and smiled.

'Grass,' said the Seabee, and curled a finger against the side of his head.

Georges swayed and pinched the bridge of his nose.

'You know?'

Georges nodded.

'We bought a few lids over – if you want some you know where to come…'

Georges nodded again and said, 'I'll stay and watch you,' but when Maude said, 'Come on!' he went quietly. 'You don't want to watch this!' Maude spread her hands and shouted, 'Come back!'

'Don't forget!' Bob yelled after them, 'Anytime.' And he went back to his work.

Other Seabees wanted to know who the natives were. A prefabricated building was erected on a rectangle of cleared land and beside this butterflies tumbled through the smoke.

Maude and the others sat in their hut and sucked beef stew out of foil packets. It was cold, and the meat gristly. Georges rolled his eyes and spilt some on his trousers. He was hungrier than ever, ate two packets and wanted more.

'No,' said Maude.

'Why not? I'm starved and there's plenty. He said we could go back for more.'

'We shouldn't have to.'

51

'But we do. Go on.' He held out a hand and fingered a piece of meat from the corner of his mouth.

'We've got to save it.'

'What's the matter with you?' Odette looked in his eyes. 'Stop looking like that.'

'Like what?' Georges stared.

'Like that!'

'I wasn't doing anything!' He shrugged and looked away.

The air was thick with the sickly smell of burning jungle. A piece of tin blew across the beach and onto the sea. The supply ship blew a cloud of smoke into the sky. Georges stood up and walked to the ruins of his hut and pissed behind it.

He'd enjoyed the joint, and a month later went back for another. Bob met him on the seaward shore beneath the runway and they watched birds swooping over the surf.

Tractors hauled trees, new lorries with working doors hauled sheets of galvanised iron as other Seabees erected fences. Frightened chickens watched from thickets, made gurgling noises and pecked at the ground. No corn, no old vegetable leaves. Dust. Fires plumed into the sky and a breeze ripped strands of smoke away. Bob rolled up, lit up and rested his head against a stump.

'You know you're not meant to be here,' he said.

'What?'

'Our boss…' Bob pointed at a prefab.

Georges grunted. He took the offered joint.

'We're taking the island over,' he said.

Georges took another toke. His brain collapsed into his stomach, he needed a drink, he tried to speak but his tongue was glued to the top of his mouth.

'Dynamite blow, huh?'

Georges nodded, and when Bob went off and came back with some more rations, he nodded again but couldn't say anything. He had to sit where he was until the feeling passed, and he could stand up and walk back to the others.

* * *

Maude went to the shop and heard that bombs were going to be exploded on the island. She told Georges. He went to meet Bob to find out if it was true, but couldn't find him. An Englishman met him instead, and told him to leave the site.

'Leave the site!'

Georges shook his head. He wanted some food. The Englishman had a red face and sweated.

'Leave the site! Go on!' He raised his voice. 'What's the matter with you?'

Georges hopped from one foot to the other. 'Bob's here?' he said.

'Look!'

'What?'

'Don't you people understand?' The Englishman wiped his brow. He waved his hands. 'You have no right to be here.'

Georges shook his head and pointed across the lagoon to where the last Ilois huts stood.

'No right.' The Englishman had a pen. He took it out of a pocket, ticked a piece of paper and walked away.

10

In September 1971, all Ilois left on Diego Garcia were called to the plantation manager's house and told that they had two weeks to pack. The manager was sad and embarrassed but he had orders. Americans had come for good. They had to have room but everything would be taken care of.

'What's to take care of?' Maude shouted.

An official looked at her and ticked a sheet of paper. 'Take it easy,' he said.

'No! The sky'll take me!' she whispered.

'What?'

'The sky. It's watching you!' She pointed at the man. He held a clipboard to his chest. 'It's watching me too, and it's remembering all this. You don't have to worry.'

'Don't I?'

'You?' said Maude. 'Oh yes, you have to worry. You means me,' she said.

'Look,' said the man. 'Talk sense.'

'I do!' Maude turned to Georges. 'Don't I?'

'Yes. Please,' he said to the official. 'She's a bit...' He shrugged. 'You know?'

'I don't!' said Maude, and stalked off. 'No, I don't.' She sang a snatch from a song, stopped in her tracks as if she'd heard someone else singing before realising it had been her, and walked on. 'I don't!' she shouted again, and waved her hands over her head.

'Touched?' said the official.

Georges shrugged.

'NO!' Odette shouted.

Bob went to visit Georges. He wanted to buy a boat. He was contracted to a long stint on the island and wanted to do some fishing. He was keen and gave the Ilois a joint. 'Smoke it later.'

Georges nodded and put it behind his ear.

'We can smoke this one now, while you tell me all about it.' He smiled and pointed at some boats on the lagoon. 'How about one of those? You won't be able to take them.' He passed the joint. 'There'll be new ones for you in Mauritius.'

'Mauritius?' said Georges.

'Sure.' Bob coughed. 'So how about it? There'd be dollars for it.' He waved some notes. 'Dollars?'

Georges didn't know about money. He shrugged and pointed to Maude. She was sitting on a tea chest. Leonard and Odette were tossing stones at a dead dog that floated in the lagoon. Other Ilois were sitting in groups around fires. Some of them drank beer. All of them had holes in their clothes.

Bob asked Maude if she wanted to sell a boat. She followed his finger when it pointed to some redundant pirogues. 'Dollars?' he said, and he rubbed his fingers together and raised his eyebrows. 'Buy yourself some clothes.'

She looked at the notes when he showed them. They were greasy and wrapped with a rubber band. 'How many?' she said.

'This many?' Bob smiled.

'You want to look?' she asked.

'Why not?'

Raphael's boat was beached beneath the hut. Its paint was flaking and a section of gunwale had come away from the hull. The sail was wrapped around the mast. Holes had appeared in the canvas, but after Bob had circled it three or four times, booted it and poked a knife in some of the planks, he said, 'Not bad. Not bad. Needs work but I've seen worse. Far worse...'

Maude sold Raphael's boat to Bob. She took his money without a word. She didn't know how much. She looked through the American. He was unnerved but forgot the feeling.

On a night in September 1971, Maude, Leonard, Odette, Georges and all remaining Ilois left Diego Garcia for ever. They leant on *The Nordvaer's* rails and watched their island disappear and glow with lights unlike lights they had seen before.

Arc lights, strings of spotlamps. Men ran to generators and aimed excavators at huts and piles of earth. A string of heavy lorries piled hills of sand beyond a spot where pumpkins had grown best. Leonard asked, 'Where are we going?'

'You ask that again and I'll throw you over,' said Odette. 'Mauritius! Mauritius!'

'I left something.'

'You didn't have anything.'

'I had my shells.'

'Those old things!' She laughed.

'My collection.'

'Forget them.'

'They took me years to find. I went everywhere. They were beautiful.'

'They were just shells,' said Odette and she sat down on a box of tractor parts.

'MY SHELLS!' Leonard shouted.

'Ssh the boy,' said Maude.

A chilly wind rattled loose fittings on the deck as Odette put her arm around her brother's shoulder. She bent her head towards him and said, 'I didn't mean to laugh.'

Leonard didn't move or speak.

'I didn't know they meant so much.'

Maude closed her eyes.

'You should have told me before. I would have brought them for you.'

Two centuries of Ilois life slipped away as the Indian Ocean heaved in massive black swells and spat over the passengers. Women cried and held their children. Men stared at the sky, gobbed and opened bottles. The few possessions they'd been allowed to keep sat in small heaps on the deck. A warship slunk past, *The Nordvaer* rolled and hooted – no reply.

Maude stayed on deck until the sky had stopped glowing with the orange and white lights that burnt on Diego Garcia. She found Georges and lay down with her head on his chest and the children by a sack of clothes. She thought about Raphael and whispered that she was, 'Coming,' before falling asleep and dreaming about winged ships crewed by donkeys and birds.

11

Raphael was happy on Grand Baie. He lived in a hut on the Perybere road, cooked fish and vegetables over an open fire, enjoyed the company of children from shacks in the field behind him and worked hard for Maurice. He became a fisherman again, and for a few months of summer felt an old self returning. He began to walk upright again, and wore a shirt he bought and new trousers someone gave him.

He thought about Maude and the children. He pictured them outside their hut on Diego, sitting on the veranda with bananas in their hands. Rose petals blew in a breeze as a pig rooted through the jungle. Georges appeared, told a joke, sat down and opened a bottle. Other Ilois walked along the beaches and lanes, half a dozen boats dotted the lagoon.

The sea rustled piles of coral. The sound of men splitting coconuts and knotting fresh nets. Heat swallowed the scene, spat it out and did the same again. Raphael spooled some line and went to bed.

In the morning, Maurice took him beyond the reef that enclosed Grand Baie and steered north east, towards the tiny islands of Coin de Mire, Ile Plate and Ilot Gabriel. The boat was powered by outboard motor, but Raphael ignored the noise and watched birds follow them, rising, drifting and tumbling out of thermals, waiting for tossed guts or heads. Maurice whistled, smoked a cigarette and held the tiller between his knees. He knew his way, what the weather was going to do, where the best fishing grounds would be, and how to open a bottle of beer with his teeth. He had stowed a box of bottles in the bows, and eyed it as he steered past Coin de Mire.

'Pass us one of those,' he said. 'And have one yourself.'

'Not me,' said Raphael. 'Not out here.' He pointed at the sea.

'You'll be alright. Here.' Maurice held his hand out.

'I'll be nothing if I do.'

Maurice nodded. He appreciated a sober crew. 'Okay,' he said, and he pointed towards Ile Plate and Ilot Gabriel.

These islands are connected by reefs. When he was close enough to hear the ocean breaking over them he turned the outboard off, cast lines and drifted for a while. He knew the waters but kept his eyes on all the signs – swell, tide, current, sky, wind, light. A lighthouse on lie Plate warns Port-Louis-bound ships to KEEP CLEAR. Dangerous seas.

The men sat back and watched their lines. The sun was hot but a cool breeze whipped the sea into little waves. They smoked cigarettes.

'You've lived here all your life?' said Raphael. He coughed. 'Grand Baie?'

'Every day. I was born in the Post Office.'

'What?'

'Yes. My mother was buying a stamp. She had a letter about medicines for the pain, but I solved that!'

'I was born on a beach,' said Raphael.

They caught enough fish for a meal. Maurice started the outboard and headed for Ilot Gabriel. 'We'll eat ashore,' he said, 'and drink.' He pointed to the bottles. 'Okay?'

'Okay.' Raphael nodded. 'Just one.'

The run to the beach was rough but Maurice had a steady hand and waited for the right waves. The two men jumped ashore, secured the boat and walked across a short stretch of sand to where grass and low scrub met the shore.

'Peaceful?' said Maurice, and Raphael nodded again.

They lit a fire, cooked the fish, drank beer and talked about boats. Ones with sails, ones with inboard motors, tourist yachts, pirogues. Later, Maurice lay back, closed his eyes and said he wanted a nap. Raphael stood up and went for a walk.

Ilot Gabriel is round, uninhabited, about a third of a mile across in any direction, and when Raphael stood at its highest point he felt it was his. All he'd ever wanted. Clean air blown from the Chagos, a boat on the beach, a friend to work for. All it needed was a hut and Maude and the children. A pig, a duck, a donkey and sixteen chickens. He could smell them. He closed his eyes. He could see them. There were no palms on the island, no trees at all, but he could plant some. They would be his, and for a few moments he became himself again – all he'd ever wanted to be.

Maurice's brother lost his job on the glass-bottom. Maurice was sorry, but he had to give him Raphael's job. He liked the Ilois, and sympathised, but loyalty to family had to come before friendship. Raphael understood. He would have done the same.

Maurice gave him twenty rupees for the trouble but there were no more jobs in Grand Baie, so he walked back to Port Louis. He had been planning to any way. He wanted to visit Alain and see if there was any news from Diego Garcia.

There was some – nothing about Maude or the children. Plenty about Americans moving in. Nothing about his boat. This depressed him. Time on Grand Baie had given him ideas, but money ran out and then he couldn't find any more work. Too many Ilois were chasing no jobs; it took less than a month for his walk to collapse. He stooped again, didn't tidy his hair and didn't mend the holes that appeared in his shirt.

'Go back to Grand Baie,' Alain urged him.

'No,' he said.

'Why not?'

'There's no more work there. Besides, I'm waiting for Maude. She'll be here soon.'

'How do you know?'

'I feel it.'

'You don't.'

'She taught me how she knew,' he said.

'Raphael!' Alain put his hands on the man's shoulders and made him look him in the eye. 'Go back to Grand Baie. There's no room here, and if you haven't got any money you can't stay.'

'Then I'll sleep in the street!'

Alain shook his head. 'No. I don't want that. People'll think I'm throwing you out. Then there'll be trouble.'

'Don't worry!' Raphael smiled. 'I'll go to the docks. You won't see me.'

Raphael met every boat that called at Port Louis, bothered loaders with questions and begged cigarettes. He shouted 'Maude!' over the heads of every group of disembarking passengers, but she never came. He let his hair grow and had days when he forgot where he was. Things he'd done blurred into each other so he wasn't sure if he was still on Grand Baie or if Alain was Maurice or Georges. The smell of roasting cummin drifted across the wharf; his stomach rumbled, he sat down, spat, and curled strings of dirt from under his fingernails with a piece of glass.

12

Maude steamed away from Diego Garcia (and Mauritius) as Raphael waited. *The Nordvaer* negotiated the treacherous shoals and currents around the Great Chagos Bank and dumped her passengers in Peros Banhos, the most southerly of the Chagos islands, 125 miles from Diego Garcia.

Peros Banhos is made up of over 30 different islands, arranged in an oblique circle to enclose 120 square miles of ocean. The transported Ilois, surprised that their destination wasn't Mauritius, looked at their new home while the Ilois whose home it was already looked back. A separate breed – Diego Garcia was a foreign country to them – but they showed the newcomers to vacant huts and gave them food and beds, knowing as much about what was going on as anyone.

Nothing; confusion spun invisible webs in the air, blocked out sense and frightened people. Children cried for no reason, bananas refused to ripen and dogs ate their puppies in frenzies with cats helping.

Peros Banhos was similar to Diego Garcia in many ways. Coconuts, fishermen, coral beaches. Its jungles weren't so tangled, though, and hid illegal dens. Toddy was brewed from fermented coconut milk in these and sold to the islanders cheap. Georges settled Maude on some sacks and went to meet a man who'd said, 'You want to taste?'

'Yes.'

'Meet me here, later?'

'I'll be here.'

He walked. He had been on the island long enough to know one's way around. Women in donkey carts nodded, others hung washing from trees. They didn't have the brooding look of Diego Garcian Ilois. No people had told them they had no right to stay. Their islands didn't enclose a perfect harbour. There was no room for an airstrip. They had heard stories from Diego Garcia and Mauritius but had plantations to tend, doormats to make and gardens to dig. The days grew shorter, stacks of firewood appeared against the walls and on the verandas of every home.

The toddy-makers were Seychellois. They kept apart from the other islanders and weren't interested in vegetable gardens, livestock, fishing or making doormats. 'Come,' one said, and took Georges' arm. 'You want to taste?'

'Yes.'

'I could tell.' He pointed. 'There's somewhere we'll go'

'Here?'

'No. Come with me.'

The Seychellois led him to a hut in a grove as a gang of mynahs screamed in breadfruit trees, took off and flew over the bay. Waves hit outcrops of rock, sprayed and fell. 'There,' said the brewer. He drained a bottle and passed a mug.

Georges drank to his people's rarity, switched from year to year, flipped dreams from hand to hand, whistled a tune, picked his nose and waited for another mug. He let thoughts rush through his head, stop, turn and turn into other thoughts. Maude – life changing – sour toddy – holes in his shoes – Leonard and Odette shouting so loud they shook coconuts from trees as ships with outriding motor boats, helicopter escorts and sailors lining rails flipped by. Flags flying. Signals. Depth charges. Jet pilots throttling up, trailing across the sky and leaving ribbons of smoke. Submarines surfacing, guns blasting.

Another mug and his face collapsed, his eyes closed, waves hit the same rocks. The mynah birds flew back. He drank until the evening, thanked the Seychellois and walked back to the others.

Leonard and Odette were talking when he got back, sat down and fell asleep. 'Georges?' said Leonard, but he got no answer.

'He's drunk,' said Odette.

'Why's he always drunk? Why doesn't he do anything?'

'He can't.'

'Father would have. He wouldn't be like that if he was with us.' Leonard pointed.

'How do you know? If someone offered him something he'd take it. But who's offering?'

'I don't know.'

'He does the best he can.'

'The best he can?' Leonard laughed but stopped when his sister shouted, 'We all do the best we can! Don't stop thinking that!'

On Peros Banhos, Odette did the best of any of them. She was eleven but older to look at and in her attitude. A straight back. Straight eyes.

'Mother?' she said.

No answer.

Maude's morbid silences and lack of interest worried Odette. She still cooked, but burnt food regularly. She never burnt food on Diego Garcia but on Peros Banhos the wind seemed to blow stronger and fan the fire uncontrollably.

'Mother? I'll be digging...'

Odette's maturity displayed itself in a vegetable garden – an old plot was attached to their hut so she borrowed a fork. She made Leonard stand with a sack to collect weeds and stones.

'Why do I have to do this?' he said.

'So we can grow vegetables. Use your head!' She pointed at her own. 'Can't you work anything out for yourself?'

'Yes. But...'

'No! One day you're complaining that Georges doesn't do anything, the next you're complaining because you have to do something!'

'I wasn't!'

'You were!'

'But...'

'Hold the sack open!'

'Alright!'

'And stop doing that!'

'I wasn't doing anything.'

Odette the boss. Leonard was older, stronger and thought he knew things but she had the mind to see beyond tomorrow, though she hadn't learnt how to see months ahead. Maude sat and stared because she had seen months ahead. The sight had blinded her, though, so everything was fugged and she felt buried. 'We'll eat this tonight,' her daughter would say, and she'd cook without thinking. Automatically, not noticing. Georges snoring off something he'd done earlier.

Odette, tired of Leonard's whingeing, said, 'Why don't you go fishing! Make a rod, find some line! I'll give you some bait. Someone'll give you a hook.'

'I haven't got a boat.'

'You don't need a boat. Look!' She pointed to someone who stood on a rock, casting into the lagoon, letting his line drift, waiting for a meal. A fish, distracted by the smell, saw the bait and took it. The fisherman struck, whipped the rod up and caught the fish as it swung out of the water towards him. 'See!' said Odette, and Leonard said, 'I suppose so.'

'Do more than that!'

'Would he mind?'

'You don't know unless you ask. Go on!'

He asked Georges to help but the man shook his head and tipped a hat over his eyes. The sun had been strong all day. He didn't want any bother. It was enough to find his way home. Children wanting to do things were a problem. 'Ask someone else.' he mumbled, and lit a cigarette. A dog strolled into the hut and out again with a piece of carrot in its mouth. Leonard said, 'Alright.'

He asked a man he found fishing the pools on the seaward side of the island. The man said, 'Why not?' and, 'I'm Paul.'

'Leonard.'

'You're from Diego.'

'You'll show me what to do?' said Leonard. He was shy, felt abroad and coughed. 'My father used to fish at home. I know some things...'

'Watch.'

Paul cut a rod from the jungle, spliced it and bound the tip, fetched some line and attached a hook. He talked about bait and taught Leonard to cast. 'Here' he said, 'flip the rod like this... wait, tug back, wait again...'

A surgeon fish waited in the shallows. It moved its body to compensate for a strengthening current, sucked at nothing and watched the surface. This moved in unpredictable eddies and ripples. The fish flashed blue scales, rose through the water and waited at a different spot.

Leonard cast. His bait hit the water and floated for a second before sinking. The fish measured the disturbance, sucked at nothing, blew and moved forwards. Eighteen inches long and fat; it flipped its tail and looked at the surface before accelerating, lunging, taking Leonard's bait, and the line screamed from the rod, picked the boy up and threw him in the water.

'WHAA!'

'Hang on!' Paul dived in and grabbed Leonard's legs. A wave smashed into them, the sea calmed, the fish pulled again.

'Hang on!' Paul shouted again.

'I am! I am!' Another wave, another tug. The man stood the boy upright and said, 'Steady! Steady...' The rod bent double. 'Head for the beach!'

'I can't.'

'You will! Come on!'

Paul helped Leonard hold the rod as they stumbled through the surf. They fell on a heap of seaweed as the fish twisted in the water and flipped out of a cloud of spindrift before breaking the line. Leonard fell on Paul, dropped his rod and yelled with laughter. He showed all his teeth. They were yellow, and brown stains traced their edges. His eyes watered. He wanted to do it again.

'Let's catch another!' he said.

'We didn't catch that one!'

'I know. But we nearly did.'

'Nearly,' said Paul, 'isn't worth anything. Nearly doesn't feed anyone. You can't go home to Mother and say, "I nearly caught a fish".'

'No, but...'

'But you did well.' Paul patted Leonard on the head. 'Well enough. You want to come again tomorrow?'

'Yes!'

'Same time?'

'I'll be here. I'll make my own rod.'

'You can keep this.' Paul handed him the one he'd made. 'A proper one.'

'A present?'

'You can call it that, if you like.'

A single bird soared over their hut and spiralled down to the trees behind it. Maude decided it meant something. Leonard came back with a bag of fish. Odette yawned and boiled a pan of lentils. 'Where've you been?' she said.

'Fishing.'

'Catch anything?'

'Yes.' Leonard held up the bag. 'Paul's good.' Odette smiled. 'Plenty,' he said.

'It was you that caught them, not Paul...'

He raised his voice. He could prove himself as easily as his sister. 'Of course!'

'Then we'll have them with tomatoes. Have a look.' She showed him a bowl.

'They're big.' Leonard smiled. 'Did you grow them?'

'What?' Odette looked at him. He winked. 'Of course I did! There's no one else!'

'Odette?'

'What?'

'I was joking.'

'Joking?'

He shrugged. 'Why not?' he said, and sat down with Maude and Georges and told them about fishing on Peros Banhos.

13

A box of clothes, a hairbrush, a bottle of aspirin. A blanket, a mirror. Odette looked at her possessions and did not believe it. She had begun to think of Peros Banhos as home. Maude wouldn't talk and Georges had done nothing but drink, but her vegetable garden was blooming. Leonard was being a fisherman. Someone yelled, 'All aboard! Move along quietly!'

They shouldered their mother up the gangplank. She was as light as a feather and unaware of what was happening. She rolled her eyes and listened to the sea lapping against the ship. She counted the number of times a wave broke. 'One, one, one, one...'

'Mother?'

'You'll earn more in a day in Mauritius than you got in a month there,' someone told everyone. 'And there'll be houses. Proper ones, not like those.' The person pointed at a row of thatched huts that nestled beneath breadfruit and coconut trees. An abandoned bicycle lay on the sand. The person cast a bow-line and went to stow some coconuts. The hold was full of them. 'So don't worry.'

'She's worried.' Odette propped her mother against a hatch. 'Look at her. She needs a doctor.'

'She'll have one in...' the person coughed, 'Mauritius.'

The Nordvaer was not built to carry more than a few passengers. The Ilois were squashed on deck and told to sit beneath tarpaulins. The sea was rough, the food they were given was off, the ship rolled badly. Women held their children to prevent them sliding overboard. Old people wailed and turned green. Georges began to curse and shake without a drink. Odette and Leonard comforted their mother and wiped her chin with a cloth as coconuts rolled across the deck and dropped through the rails.

The Ilois were surprised to find themselves dumped in the Seychelles, but the cargo of coconuts had to be unloaded so they were ordered off, counted, vaccinated and shown through customs and immigration. No one told them what to do or where to go.

In desperation, they walked to the offices of the uncle of the last plantation manager on Diego Garcia. This man tried to find somewhere for them to say. He phoned and sent runners to local hostels, and asked officials from the Seychelles Government to help.

'But Ilois are British subjects,' they said. 'They're the responsibility of BIOT.'

A BIOT administrator was called. He suggested that the Ilois could stay in a local prison.

Odette and the others bedded down in cells. Some prisoners served them their first proper meal in days. The place stank of piss and rotten eggs.

'What you in for?' said a thief.

'Me?' said Georges.

'Yes.'

'Nothing. I haven't done anything.'

The prisoner grinned. 'No. Neither have I!' He laughed and ladelled some rice onto his plate.

'No. I mean it.'

'So do I! Really! Ask anyone. I wasn't anywhere near the house. The bloke that did it's living on Praslin. I was nowhere near.'

'No?'

'But I got five years! I ask you.' The man crouched down and whispered. 'When I get out my first stop's that bastard. He thinks Praslin far enough away!' He clenched his fist. 'See that?'

Georges nodded.

The man stood up and laughed. 'Good for you!'

The sound of doors slamming and orders ringing down corridors interrupted them.

'HEY!'

'SIR!'

'SWEEP THAT UP!'

'SIR!'

'AND WHEN YOU'VE FINISHED, WASH THE BROOM AND REPORT TO ME! BRING A SHOVEL!'

'SIR!'

'I'VE GOT ANOTHER LITTLE JOB FOR YOU! SOMETHING YOU'LL ENJOY VERY MUCH.'

'SIR!'

'YOU LIKE WORKING HERE, DON'T YOU?'

'OH YES SIR.'

A door slammed. Keys jangled.

'How about a drink?' said Georges.

'Sure!' The prisoner left.

Georges waited. A drink. He bit a fingernail as he waited. The prisoner came back with a jug of water.

'No,' said Georges. 'A real drink!'

The prisoner laughed again. 'Oh sure,' he said, and left the jug on the floor. 'Sure!'

'I thought you...'

'Go to sleep.'

Odette screwed her eyes tight and refused to listen. They were locked in at nine o'clock but lights and noise from the streets kept them awake. The sound of cars and people meeting each other, talking about the usual things people talk about on warm streets in the evening. Bars were open.

Nine days later, the Ilois were taken from their cells and counted back onto *The Nordvaer*. Her cargo had been unloaded. The weather was hot, palm trees nodded over sweeps of blinding sand. The sun stung the roads and the air filled with the smell of melting tar as she nudged her way out of harbour and set course for Mauritius.

14

Raphael gave up waiting, slipped very quickly and ended up sitting in a doorway and begging. He slept in a ditch on the road to Beau Bassin.

All he'd ever wanted to be was what he'd been but now his nose dripped and his mind was bowled by hazed memories, swinging backwards and forwards and back again. The distant sound of waves breaking on a reef came, stayed for a second and went. Tourists saw him, folded their arms and said, 'Well of course they do it because they want to.' He held out a hand but no one gave him a coin. He wanted to die.

'Why don't they go home?' said Mauritians. 'They don't like it here.'

'No…'

'They've got their own place.'

'The Chagos.'

'It's beautiful there.'

Raphael had no shoes. His last pair had broken. He left them by a drain and walked barefoot.

People stepped off the pavement to avoid him. He smelt. His hair was dirty and his face covered in scabs. He pissed his pants and sat down again.

A dog sniffed him, yelped and jumped away. His torn trousers exposed sores on his knees and feet. A policeman shook him by the shoulder.

'Hey!'

Raphael groaned.

'Up! You're blocking the way.'

'I'm getting up.'

What Raphael saw swam. He was starving. His stomach

ballooned, the light hurt his eyes, all he'd been able to shit for a fortnight was blood.

The movement of traffic confused him. The smell of a roasting chicken made him cry. He mumbled about fishing and hooks, the policeman helped him up. Passers-by shook their heads and asked each other questions. Beggars were beggars but people who came from a paradise to be beggars and not go back made them scratch their heads. 'It's very beautiful there.'

'We learnt about them in school.'

Raphael disappeared into a side-street. It was damp but no one bothered him there. He lay down beside a pile of tyres. A rat crawled over his chest, sniffed his coat and gnawed a corner of it. Steam spewed out of a restaurant window and drifted in clots down the street.

Raphael took shallow breaths, licked his lips and squinted at the wall opposite him. A torn poster advertised a film. He had never been in a cinema, didn't know what the word meant. He had seen televisions switched on in rows in a shop; he had stood and watched for a minute, but confused and with his mouth taut had walked away and sat outside a church.

Raphael closed his eyes and his mouth. His skin was dry and a graze on his cheek hadn't healed. It wept; he didn't scratch it.

He smelt a copra factory and the hanging scents of the jungle plantations. Children calling for someone. The noise of a sheet of canvas flapping over a veranda. Maude mending a shirt on the veranda, the lights of East Point flitting through haze.

Maude talking to Leonard. 'Sweep the floor and take the rubbish away. Be a good boy...' Odette taking the broom before her brother stood up, swatting him with it and running down to the beach. Maude shouting, 'Come back with it!' but shrugging and turning away from her children. Raphael saw himself in the Chagos Archipelago waiting for a tide to fall... the clatter of saucepans from the restaurant and another blast of steam brought him round. He opened his eyes, squinted at the wall opposite and moved.

Raphael moved only once more before he died. He moved his head to make himself more comfortable. The sun set with a slur of light and it began to rain. His body was found the next day by a Chinese cook. After a designated period of time during which no one came forward to claim him, he was buried in an unmarked grave by a priest who was late for something he'd already had to put off twice. A week later, *The Nordvaer* arrived in Mauritius, and Odette and the others disembarked.

15

In Mauritius, Maude's intuitions warned her of death stalking the slums of Port Louis. They pointed to the traffic, the tall buildings, and the mountains that ring the city. They were covered in scrub, black where rocks showed through, and higher than she'd imagined height could go. They panicked her.

She felt Raphael. His smell and presence filled her body. She saw him dead, like in the open drains that ran down the streets around her shack. Dead dogs often blocked them, and other dogs would nose and bother the corpses.

Death was also on the rags people washed and spread to dry over tin sheets. With no trees and the wash of the sea further away than it had ever been before, and the rumble of cars and lorries all night, Maude held her hands over her ears and rocked in the dark.

Leonard and Odette sat up and watched her by the light of the moon. She lay with her arms at awkward angles. Dogs howled. Other people in shacks along the street tossed and moaned.

A cock crowed. A baby cried. An unlatched door banged against a bucket. The baby's mother didn't have any milk. The shock of the final move had dried her.

A pile of rags, an empty oil barrel, a roll of rusty wire standing on a stretch of waste ground. Children playing in a cesspool.

And death was in the midday sun when the shade of a favourite tree was missing, and all Maude had was shadow cast by shacks. No chickens to feed, no garden to weed or palm leaves to cut and freshen the hedge with. She narrowed her eyes and went to find Raphael. She tuned her senses and sniffed the air.

It stank of rotten fruit, sweating people, dirty clothes and rank dogs with limps. Traffic fumes and decomposing rats. She concentrated, held her breath, whispered, 'Raphael,' and walked away from the slums towards the docks.

'Hello?'

He was strong at the docks. Sailors called to her and cars hooted but she looked straight ahead, knowing he had been there. She found a doorway, clenched a fist to her forehead and could almost touch his face. It was cold but it was his – his lips moved, she moved, the presence moved to another doorway and then sat on a wharf and watched the sea lap against the harbour walls.

Cargo ships and tugs. Maude joined him. 'Raphael?' she said. She nodded at imagined responses. 'I knew you'd wait. You…' she coughed, 'you were always good at waiting.'

Maude began to cry. Her tears ran down her face. 'Because we came,' she spluttered. 'Didn't we?' She raised her voice. 'Didn't we?' She looked around. 'Are you going to answer me?'

The tears came from a great lake in her body, pumped through pipes lined with glass. She tasted them and spat, 'DIDN'T WE?' she screamed.

A policeman heard her. He approached. She said, 'We came and now you're like this. Why are you like this? It's no good. You can't help, so why bother me?'

'Hello,' said the policeman. He was a patient man, and recognised the woman as Ilois. 'You shouldn't sit on the edge.'

Maude didn't move.

'Hello?'

'What do you want?'

'You shouldn't sit so close to the edge. You'll fall.' He stretched a hand out to her.

Maude gripped the metal runner that ran the length of the edge of the wharf and said, 'We came but he couldn't wait.' She didn't look at the policeman.

'Who couldn't wait?'

'Him.'

'Who was he?'

Maude put a hand to her forehead. 'He was a stupid man,' she said softly, and sobbed. 'Stupid.'

'I don't think he was.' He shook his head. 'Not if you're like this because of him.'

Maude turned around. She looked at the man. The buttons of his jacket shone. His face was pockmarked. She nodded. 'Yes,' she mumbled, and turned away.

The policeman helped Maude to stand up. Her bones cracked. He could feel them through her clothes. 'When did you last eat?' he said.

She didn't know. She shook her head and leant against him. His body was warm. She wanted to stay there. He moved. 'Come on,' he said. 'I'll take you home.'

She couldn't remember where she lived but he knew roughly. The Ilois were well known to the police, but no special orders had been issued. Everything was secret; everything was wrapped and sealed.

'Stop,' Maude said, and leant against a wall. She stroked some bricks.

'Why?'

'He's strong here.' She sniffed. 'Very strong.'

'Who's strong?'

'I can smell him. I can! Here!' She pointed at the wall. 'Didn't I tell you?'

'What?' The policeman couldn't see anything.

'Raphael! He's everywhere!'

'Look.' The policeman wouldn't lose his temper, but he had other things to do. 'You'll feel better at home.'

'I feel better here.'

'No.' He took Maude's arm, pointed and led her on. 'We'll be there soon.'

Maude lived in a slum – Roche Bois – in Port Louis. Dogs barked at their approach. 'Which one?' said the policeman, and pointed to shacks. 'Do you remember?'

'No.'

'You have friends here, though?'

'Friends?' Maude didn't know. She stopped and looked around. 'There are many people here.'

'I know,' said the policeman.

Leonard and Odette had been looking for their mother. They'd walked in every direction and asked everyone they knew, but no one had seen her.

'She's about this high.' Odette indicated with her hand.

'And doesn't talk much,' said Leonard. 'Not like she used to. She used to.'

People shook their heads. Odette was leading her brother home when they saw a policeman. 'We'll ask him,' she said.

A week later, with Maude so confused you could thread string through her teeth and play music with it and her lips, Georges went off. He found dollars left from the money Bob had paid for Raphael's boat, took them and bought rum and cigarettes from a Chinese shop.

'You're thirsty?'

Georges shook his head.

'Where did you get dollars?'

Georges shrugged, left the shop, walked out of Port Louis and took the road to Beau Bassin. A road-mender told him not to walk in the traffic and a man on a motorcycle swore at him. Clouds swept in from the sea and cooled the sun, the humidity increased and Georges left his shoes on the pavement outside a church before walking into a wrecking yard full of broken buses.

There was no one about. He wandered around piled tyres and stripped chassis. He didn't know what to do. Mauritius was a mystery to him. On Diego Garcia he'd been told what to do and hoped that one day Maude would come round to his way of thinking. She'd always been special, but to look at her now – he thought. To look at her now. He didn't want to. She hadn't noticed him for months. 'Raphael's about,' she'd say. 'Coming Raphael.' He kicked a tin can, lit a cigarette and sat on a tyre.

The cloud thickened. The sun disappeared completely. It started to rain. Sudden massive drops bucketed from the sky and turned the dust to mud. They put his cigarette out. It sagged before disintegrating and dropping into the mud. He took a mouthful of rum and wiped his lips with the back of his hand.

He sat through the storm with his mouth open, letting it fill with water and dribble down his front. He got lost in it and didn't move. A big man; once he'd been able to stare coconuts out of trees and charm birds. Now he rolled his eyes and didn't want the rain to stop. It reminded him and took him back like Ilois were constantly being taken back. Memories were all they had to look forward to – a familiar bed and a string of washed huts along a road through the jungle. The burst of ocean over coralline beaches or the smell of a pan of boiling lobsters.

Two donkeys eating lettuce.

Five dead ducks hanging from a veranda pole.

Two dogs with a couple of boys and a football.

A cat chasing beetles through the jungle. Eleven chickens bursting out of cover, running down the beach, backing off when they met the water, running back up the beach to the cover, not asking themselves why they had burst out of it in the first place.

A shift of rats belting down the lane and his mother pouring calou. A mug. He wanted a drink.

When the storm passed, he sat in a pool of water for an hour before standing up and walking towards Beau Bassin. He begged his way there, managed enough money for a bottle of beer before heading south, towards Curepipe. He stayed there for six months, working the bus station, before moving on to Mahebourg.

'You should go with her,' said Odette, talking to Leonard about their mother.

'She won't let me.'

'Won't let you?'

'She says she wants to walk on her own.'

'Then follow her without her noticing.' Odette was worried. 'Every time she goes out she gets lost. Someone's got to watch her.'

'Why don't you?'

'Leonard! What are you talking about? I've got enough to do!' She spread her arms at the shack. 'You do nothing!'

'I beg!'

'We all beg! But what do you do for her? Cook food? Fetch water? Keep the roof down?'

'You always do those things anyway...'

Odette laughed. To hear her reminded Leonard of a crow. Maude, dozing in a corner, woke up.

'He's about,' she whispered, opened her eyes wide and sneezed. She wasn't talking about Georges. He had been gone a long time. No one had had the energy to find out what had happened. It was enough to keep the roof down. Ilois disappeared every day and never came back. Ilois were illiterate in a country full of readers and writers. Port Louis was a big city. Maude sneezed again.

She had a cold. She'd never had a cold before. Snot was caked around her nostrils and over her top lip. She picked some away and ate it. 'He is,' she said, and stood up.

'You going out?' said Odette.

Maude stopped, surprised by the voice. She turned around and looked at her daughter as if she didn't recognise her. 'Out?' she said. 'Of course.'

Odette prodded her brother. 'Leonard'll come with you,' she said.

'Leonard?'

'Yes.'

'Leonard...' She narrowed her eyes and looked at the boy. He was skinny and narrow-headed. He didn't smile, his eyes were dull and his skin was tight. 'No,' she said. 'I don't think so. I'll go on my own,' and she left the shack.

'Follow her!' Odette was ordering. She was tired of policemen bringing her home. She held herself straight. Her eyes would refuse to dull. She pointed down the street and said, 'Go on! Hurry!'

Leonard went.

He followed his mother at a distance. He dodged into side streets and doorways. She kept stopping and looking over her shoulder. He didn't know enough about his mother to know that her second sight was stronger than it had ever been. She could feel his eyes in her back. She let him think she was unaware for ten more minutes before diving into a shop, waiting for him to catch up and jumping out.

'Boy!' she said, and cackled.

'Mother!'

'Think I didn't know you were there?' She took his arm and walked on.

'No...' he said, 'but you made me jump, coming out like that.'

'Ha!' She rolled her eyes and said, 'Did I?'

'Yes.'

They walked towards the docks.

'Why aren't you more like your father?'

'I...'

'Odette's more like him than you are. That's not right.'

'Odette just knows more things.'

'No, she doesn't. She just doesn't let things she does know bother her. You should be like that...'

Leonard looked at his mother and wondered how she could talk. Talk about being bothered.

'...he'd have wanted that,' she said.

'Who?'

'There you go again!' She sneezed and spat across the road. 'Who! And you're still young. Look at me! I can't...' She stopped in mid-sentence, wiped her nose on her sleeve and sniffed. 'He's always strong here,' and she went to the entrance to a side street and rubbed a wall there. 'Feel him?'

Leonard shrugged.

Maude shrugged. 'No,' she said. 'You wouldn't,' and she sat on the pavement, held a hand out and looked up at passers-by.

'I'll go across,' said Leonard, and pointed. He might have been slow, but he knew enough not to beg too close to another. 'Space yourselves,' people had said. He squatted outside the post office, collected three cents in two hours and walked home alone.

16

One Tuesday, Odette begged seventy-five cents, cooked a meal of boiled fish and carrots, collected eight buckets of water, four bundles of scrap wood and chopped it. Leonard begged ten cents, watched his mother for a few hours, talked with her for ten minutes and helped Odette find some rope. Maude begged nothing, and felt her husband hang over her like a huge leaf, or a steady, personal shower of rain.

On Diego Garcia he had smelt of fish, salt, sweat and hair, a hint of woodsmoke and sometimes rum. Never much. Unlike other Ilois men, he'd always been careful with drink. He believed that the sea could smell drink. It would get jealous; drown a two-timing man. 'You never know,' he'd say, and sometimes stroke her hair or her cheek.

She stroked her own cheek. Odette watched for a moment before going outside, kneeling over a pile of sticks and striking a match. She fanned flames, fetched a pot of water and set it on a square of bricks around the fire.

Leonard was in disgrace. He sat on a wall by a wheelless car and shared a cigarette with other boys. He didn't notice the weather and didn't know what day it was. He wanted to but other things blocked his mind. Food, drink, clothes. Clothes were why he was in disgrace. His sister was ashamed of him, all his mother could say was, 'Is it cooked?' A short story.

He'd walked into Port Louis. He rubbed his stomach, picked his teeth and nodded at women by taps and children carrying baskets to school. People on buses, policemen directing traffic. He counted cars, the sun was hot all day.

He sat under the royal palms on Place d'Armes, enjoyed the shade and admired the clothes smart people wore. Bankers, merchants and civil servants. Officials in long cars swept into Government House. He watched them.

He was joined in the shade by a man who unwrapped an ice cream and sucked it. 'Lick?' he said to Leonard.

'Me?'

'Sure.'

'Okay. Thanks.' Leonard wiped his mouth. 'Thanks,' he said again, and licked.

The man asked questions. Leonard didn't have any answers. All he knew was his name, the name of his home, the few things Paul taught him on Peros Banhos, the few things Odette and his mother had shown him, the fact that Ilois couldn't go home. 'I don't know,' he said.

'But you live in Port Louis?'

Leonard nodded.

'And you're Mauritian?'

'No. I don't think so. If you wanted to know, really, you'd have to ask my sister. She knows.'

'Your sister?'

'Yes.'

Leonard looked at the man and wondered why he was asking questions and sharing his ice cream. He asked him, 'Why you want to know?'

'Just curious…'

'Curious?'

'Sure.'

'Why?'

'I like to know about people.' The man bit a piece of the ice cream and chewed it. 'It's my hobby.'

'Hobby?' Leonard didn't know the word. 'Where is your hobby?'

'Where? It's not anywhere.'

'Then…' said Leonard, but didn't know how to finish. He had feelings about the man. He stood up. 'Then I have to go, anyway.'

'Goodbye, then.'

'Goodbye.'

He crossed the road and cut down an alley to the market. On Diego Garcia you could rely on people not to be strange. Port Louis was full of different people, but he couldn't understand why about anything; Ilois couldn't. However many times they asked questions about home, no official person gave them a word, or came to visit them in their shacks.

Leonard idled his way between market stalls. Many different types of goods were for sale. Racks hung with kitchen utensils, baskets full of chickens, tables of herbs and spices. Busy women picked their way through fruits and vegetables, children yelled at each other and squashed discarded tomatoes. Shirts and trousers hung from rails, T-shirts for tourists and dresses. Leonard's eye was caught by a dress.

It was red and swung from a wire hanger. Other dresses hung on the same rail but it stood out. It wasn't patterned, but its colour appealed to him. He couldn't understand why – no different from any other time or thing – he went to it and touched its shoulder.

Cotton. Three buttons down the front. A shiny belt for the waist. He fingered it and looked around. No one was minding the shop.

He stole it in a flash. He didn't think. He'd never stolen before. He crumpled it up, stuck it up his shirt and ran away, through the crowds.

Mothers with babies got in his way, traders carrying trays of cakes stopped to let him pass. A policeman shook his head and rolled his eyes. No one yelled, 'Stop thief!' No one noticed a thing. Market was where anything went on. One man running was as good as another.

He reached Roche Bois before daring to take the dress out and smooth it down. He smiled at it. Odette's size. Odette's present. She kept him and their mother alive. He had to do something. He had done something. He laughed and grinned from ear to ear when he gave it to her.

'Where did you get it?'

'Market!'

'But, but you couldn't have enough money for something like this.' She flicked it. 'How did you…'

'I took it. It was…'

'Took it? What do you mean? You can't just take things! Did you pay for it?'

'No. But…'

'But you stole it!' She brushed a mark off the dress. 'That's what you mean, isn't it?'

Leonard nodded. He should have known better. 'Yes.'

'Then take it back!'

'But…'

'Take it back!' She stamped her feet. 'Go on!'

Leonard wanted to say something about how their home had been stolen. He wanted to point at the rags she wore and say that one dress from so many didn't matter, but he couldn't. He walked back to the market and left it hanging on the entrance gates. It flapped there, more like some flag than clothes.

Odette didn't call him for food. She decided to let him stay on the wall. Maude could eat his share. She deserved it. She sneezed.

'You want some fish?'

'Is it cooked?'

'Of course it's cooked! There's rice too.'

'I'll call Leonard.'

'No! Leave him. He can get his own.'

Maude shrugged. She would let her daughter decide. She had done enough for one day – days rattled through her head like bones and she saw Raphael behind her eyes. She said, 'He won't be eating either,' and chewed some fish.

17

If, between December and April, strong northerly trade winds meet gusting southerly trade winds, cyclones are likely to swing in banana-shaped paths across the length of the Indian Ocean. Oppressive heat and a deathly stillness are the first signs of one's approach. Dogs wilt, roads melt at the edges. Cyclone Gervaise followed the classic pattern.

'Help me,' said Odette. She was carrying two buckets of water and stopped to get her breath back. She took a corner of her skirt and wiped her face with it. Leonard didn't move. 'HEY! LEONARD!'

He looked up, sulking. His hair had grown and hung in his eyes. On Diego Garcia, his mother had given him a regular haircut. 'What?' he said.

'You can carry that one,' and she left one of the buckets in the street.

He made a face but did as his sister said. He put the bucket in the shack and said, 'Alright?' to his mother.

She didn't respond. The weather was upsetting. She didn't like the closeness. She thought the air was trying to strangle her, the stillness grabbed sound and stifled it. Her cold had gone but a cough replaced it. She coughed.

Leonard hadn't forgotten that she was his mother, but too many times some mood got in the way. He knew he should do more, but – he thought – he was still a boy. Odette was still a girl. He shook his head, thinking that a girl shouldn't have to work so hard.

Two days later, Gervaise cruised off the ocean and wheeled across Mauritius. It tossed rocks that kept roofs down and threw galvanised walls, empty oil barrels, trees, goats and cars into ditches. Houses collapsed, boats sunk, rivers burst their banks, the rain poured in solid blocks a mile square and three miles high. Bus timetables were suspended and warnings issued by the meteorological office at regular intervals. Roche Bois was flattened. Odette and Leonard carried their mother outside and laid her in the street.

The Ilois had never seen anything like it. Diego Garcia had been outside the cyclone area, sandwiched between the equatorial current and the Indian counter current; the worst weather there had been rain storms. Sometimes the wind picked up for a few days, but died down quickly.

Maude bled from a cut to her forehead. A sheet of tin had hit her. She dabbed her fingers over the wound, tasted blood and said, 'Salty,' to Odette.

Other people carried dead people down the street. Children wailed, ambulances and police-cars sirened between hospitals and the shanties as firemen trained hoses on fires and workmen attached grapples to the sides of ruined shacks.

'Salty,' she said, and the scales fell from her eyes. She could see everything exactly. Uncleared cyclone rubble was piled in the streets she walked. Raphael's spirit stopped haunting her. One day she was exploring his old stamping grounds, leaning on walls and sitting on boxes in side streets; the following morning, she woke up and said, 'He's dead,' and meant it. 'Gone,' and she stood up straight.

Odette had forgotten how tall her mother was. She said, 'He went years ago.'

'Did he?' Maude put a hand over her mouth. 'What's the matter, Odette?'

'You look… look well. Your face is different.'

'It is different,' she said, 'and I feel different. Yes!' And she went outside.

The air was thick. She patted a dog, and when Odette prodded Leonard into following her, she said, 'No. Not now. I'm going on my own. Don't follow me today.'

Leonard shrugged and looked at his sister. 'Bye then,' he said and went to sit on a wall.

He didn't watch his mother walk away; Odette did. She had more of her mother's intuition than she knew. She lifted a hand to wave but it stuck in mid-air without moving; it clenched into a fist; Maude rounded the corner and disappeared from sight.

She didn't mean to catch a bus but was standing by a stop when one came along, so she got on. The conductor asked her where she was going. She shrugged.

'Rupees?' he said.

'Here,' she said, and took three fifty cent pieces from her pocket.

'One rupee to Pamplemousses. You want to go there?'

'Pamplemousses?'

'Yes.'

'I don't know.'

'Look!' The conductor was impatient. Other passengers hadn't paid their fares, and the bus would stop again soon. An inspector was lurking. 'Pamplemousses?'

Maude shrugged. 'Okay,' and she let him take the coins from her hand. She took the ticket but didn't know what to do with it, so she screwed it up and dropped it on the floor.

The bus left Port Louis behind. Pepinere, Le Hochet. At Terre Rouge, the road forked. Three goats were sitting in the triangle of dust formed by the junction of roads, and chewed while traffic sped around them. One scratched and stood up, waited for a gap between two lorries, and walked across the road. It bit a hedge and sat down in someone's garden. Children played in a school playground, priests left a mosque in solemn groups.

A policeman on a moped with a leather satchel tied to the front mudguard, overtook the bus, waved to the driver and accelerated away. Two old women stood in a doorway with baskets on their heads.

Half-built concrete houses, piles of rubble left in Gervaise's wake, broken lorries parked on verges. Shops selling fruit, beer and cakes. Small men working at sewing machines in the open air.

Maude watched these things, and needed reminding when the bus reached Pamplemousses. The conductor helped her off. The driver shook his head. One of her breasts had fallen through a hole in her dress. She tucked it back in, and didn't watch for traffic when she crossed the road.

Pamplemousses is famous for its Botanical Garden. This contains one of the finest collections of tropical plants and palms on earth, and enjoys a worldwide reputation. Maude stood in front of its gates and watched as tourists avoided the hawkers and boys. They yelled, 'Hey!'

'What?' (said a tourist).

'You want guide?'

'No. We'll find our own way round.'

'No! You need guide. I am guide. I can show places you don't know unless!'

'Unless what?'

'Unless I'm your guide!'

'Look! Can't you read?' Signs stated 'There is no official guide to the gardens. Entrance is free.'

Maude couldn't read. No hawkers bothered her. She walked through the gates, and along a broad avenue of massive palms.

Narrow paths led off the main avenue, through trees and beside lakes and ornamental ponds. Tunnels of greenery dripped coolness in every season; Maude sat on a stone bench beneath a portico of flame trees.

Her mind was very clear; she knew who she was and where she was, where she had come from and how her husband had died. She knew her son was called Leonard and her daughter Odette. She closed her eyes, listened to the sound of the wind playing in the trees, and smelt flowers. The gentle gurgle of a stream, the voices of passing guides…

'These are the famous Victoria Regia lilies. They can support the weight of a small child! Further on we see the Fan Palm, or Talipot. This tree blooms only once, and then only after one hundred years. Then it dies!'

'Here we have the celebrated Gourami fish. If you wish to pull some grass and toss it in the pond, you'll be able to observe them eating the grass.'

'This tree was planted by Princess Margaret of England.'

'These deer are descended from the original Java deer introduced to Mauritius by the Dutch.'

'These giant tortoises are over one hundred years old. Originally, they came from Aldabra, a group of islands situated north west of Malagasy.'

A gardener, walking home after a long day up an olive tree with a knife (his own property), passed the portico where Maude sat. He was a small man, tired and smelling the roasting lamb his wife would be cooking. She cooked outside, under a mango tree with all her children counted and waiting. She covered her hair with a shawl, adjusted it in line with her fringe and sang a song she'd been taught in school. She'd been a child in Port Louis but preferred Pamplemousses.

The gardener leant against a tree and took deep breaths. He wasn't a talker. Botanists often asked him questions but he always feigned ignorance or deafness. He was paid to tend the gardens, knew they were famous and knew he was lucky to work in the shade; he nodded good night to another gardener and took a cigarette out of his pocket.

He turned around and struck a match on a trunk of a Talipot palm. He squinted, inhaled and tossed the match in the portico. He saw Maude and walked towards her.

'Hey!' he said.

Maude did not move.

'Hey! We're closing now. Time to go home.' He went to her and shook her. She was stiff but her eyes were open. He jumped back when she fell off the bench. She had been dead for three hours.

She lay on the ground as if she was still sitting. Flies buzzed around her nose and drank the fluids that ran from her eyes. The gardener stared at her for a minute before going for help.

When she was carried away, he remarked that she was as light as a child, and when a policeman asked him to sign a form stating that he was the finder of the body, he smoothed his hair, felt proud and wished his family could see him.

18

Maude left an atmosphere in the Roche Bois shack. It bled from the walls as a palm tree, a man mending thatch, a chicken and an enormous sun throwing speaking beams of light across a foamed and spent ocean. 'I'm not staying here,' said Leonard – the most positive thing he'd ever said.

'Nor am I.'

'We'll move.'

They carried their possessions away and found a shack on the edge of Cassis. The main Port Louis–Moka highway ran twenty-five yards from the door and an old woman stood on a stretch of waste ground, rocking backwards and forwards on her heels. She wore a grey cardigan in all weathers. No one knew who she was or where she slept, but she collected coins thrown from passing cars.

'This is better than Roche Bois,' said Leonard. He pointed to the few concrete buildings growing up amongst the corrugated. 'We'll stay here.'

Odette nodded.

'There's more room.'

'That's because we're on our own.'

'There's still more room.'

Their shack had no windows, but a few sheets of tin, bent and nailed to its front served as a veranda. Odette arranged some wire over a square of bricks and lit a fire.

'How'd you like to give boys a good time?'

'A good time?' Odette didn't know.

'Sure.'

'I don't know.'

'Well look. I'm Marie. You think about it. I'm always around.

You'll see me.'

The new shack was free of their mother's spirit, but nothing else changed. Weeks of begging and scrounging became months; down by the bus station, outside airline offices, at the bottom of the museum and library steps, in the parks or around the docks. Some days were good, others not. One week in July, all they could manage was twenty cents and two ripe bananas and Leonard spent the weekend on the floor of the shack, holding his stomach. He couldn't get up. His decisiveness following Maude's death had gone.

Odette looked at him. For a while she'd thought he was changing and taking the pressure off, but then he didn't care any more. She had to prop him up and make him comfortable.

'Leonard?' she said.

'What?' He wasn't dying but his voice was weak.

'Have some of this.' She had a cup of water. He sipped. 'I'm going out now,' she said.

'Out?'

'Yes.'

'Where?'

'The docks. I'll bring something back.'

Leonard nodded, but didn't watch her leave.

Marie hung around the docks and waited for girls like Odette. She had said, 'How you like to give boys a good time?' so many times that the words had stained her teeth. A smart woman, eyeing dollars/pounds/rupees and poor girls with one thing to sell; she'd approached Odette before. But Ilois women were slow to understand their value. On Diego Garcia, sex had not been sold. '… a good time?'

'Sure.'

'I don't know…'

'For money…' Marie looked Odette in the eye. She had a persuasive mouth and pursed it.

'Money?'

'Sure. Sometimes forty, fifty rupees.'

'No!'

'Some girls do.'

'Who?'

Marie gave Odette the names of some girls she knew.

'They don't!'

'They do. Ask them!'

The next day, with Leonard up but still weak, she asked around.

'Don't you?'

'No...'

'And with a face like that. And your body!'

She wondered what she was going to do, looked at her brother and wondered the same about him. He worried but never wondered. She wondered, worried, waited. Dogs barked, a sulky moon hung in the sky. She stared at it. They hadn't eaten for two days. Every time they breathed they rattled.

'Sure. Sometimes, forty, fifty rupees.' Fifty rupees. Once. She might do it, forget it, not worry. A week later, she crept out to meet Marie. 'Any time,' the woman had said. 'I'll show you.'

'Most of them are too excited. Some don't even get as far as you. Half a minute...' Marie cut the air with her hand, 'and it's over. No problem.'

'So quick?'

'Sure.'

'Why?'

Marie laughed. 'Because they're men! Don't you know anything?'

Odette nodded. 'Yes, but...'

But hungry to nod again. Money was a big word. She was nervous and stopped walking.

'What's the matter?'

'I...' she stuttered.

'Look. Odette.' Marie took the girl's face in her hand and stared into her eyes. 'Just stick by me.'

A long street. Single lights pricked the dark, shacks and houses were built close together. Puddles. Alleys. Shadowed women who knew what they were doing. Sailors and other men with money holding bottles, standing in groups, yelling at other groups. Loud music from dark buildings.

Marie stood Odette in a doorway. Iron grills covered the windows of the shop it served. A rat scuttled across the street with something in its mouth. The moon came out. A man approached.

'You!' He pointed at Odette. 'How about it?'

'How about what?' said Marie.

'I'm talking to her.' The man's face was shaded by a hat. He smelt of diesel oil. He rolled a cigarette.

'And I'm her friend.'

'And her pimp? How about two of you,' the man licked his lips, 'together?'

'What?'

'You heard.'

Marie stroked her chin. Odette tried to look small but when Marie said, 'Come on then,' to the man and took her arm, she didn't worry or wonder.

A minute. Another woman and a sailor called Jack. One night in a first-floor room, dirty windows and a single light bulb. Other people in other rooms pounded away as a fight started in the street outside. The sound of a siren and a ship's hooter. The wink of traffic lights, the clank of two people riding one bicycle. Odette kept her eyes closed and her body rigid, ground her teeth together but couldn't stifle a single scream. A sharp one in the night and then he finished and gave Marie thirty rupees.

'Thirty?' Odette said. They were back on the street.

'There's ten for you,' said Marie. She held one nostril and shot a gob of snot from the other.

'Ten! But you said fifty and...'

'Fifty!' Marie shook her head. 'You've got a lot to learn.'

'But...' Odette bled. She held herself. She started to cry. 'I thought...' She sniffed. 'Fifty. I could have bought enough food and...' Her voice broke. Her heart fainted.

'You've got ten.'

The note was in her hand. She looked at it. It was wet. There was a picture of the Queen on it. 'But…' she said again.

'Odette!' Marie gave her one hard look. 'If you want that sort of money you work the hotels. You can't earn that down here.'

'What hotels?'

'On the coast. But you need more than just a body for that.'

'But fifty rupees…'

'Forget it, Odette.'

That sort of money. When Odette got home, she stripped and stood behind the shack in a basin of water. She had a rag and washed herself for an hour. She didn't get to bed until four, but couldn't sleep. Leonard was snoring, a bad moon sank.

Ten rupees. In the morning, he stood up and asked where she'd got it.

'I begged it.'

'Where?'

'At market. It was busy.'

'It's always busy!'

'Busier then,' she whispered.

He believed her. It was lots of money but her eyes could plead. She always collected more than him. He didn't have the touch or look. He would sit on his wall. If Odette could beg enough to live on, why should he do anything? There was nothing to do anyway; the wall was comfortable.

He didn't notice when the money ran out and Odette begun to stay out late once in every three nights. But Marie had shown her all she needed to know. She had to pray that an image of her mother's face didn't appear but if she closed her eyes, gritted her teeth, held her arms against the side of her body and waited it was over. She earned fifteen rupees a time, washed herself carefully and bought a hairbrush with a blue back. It was hers. She hid it from her brother in a gutter and used it when he was asleep.

An American called Dan picked her up. He'd come from San Francisco on a supply ship out of Subic Bay. He spoke quietly. 'It's a helluva way from the States. God; I feel it.' He scratched his face.

'What?'

'Oh, I don't know. Homesick? I guess that's it. Sick, anyway.'

'You want to do something with me?'

'Sure. Let's talk for a while, then...'

'Talk?'

'Sure.'

'I haven't got anything to say.'

'Listen then honey, okay?'

'Okay.'

Dan was a thin man and he rolled his eyes as he talked about home. He talked about his wife. He had a poetic streak. He called her a 'cat in a fish'. He talked about his job. His ship was in dock for ten days.

'You've seen many countries?'

'Lots,' he said. He had a bottle of rum and poured some. 'You name it, I've been there.' He drank.

He talked about Europe and America, and impressed her with stories about shops and buildings. Australia, the Philippines, Hawaii, Japan. 'You ever been to Japan?' he said, then, 'No, of course not.'

She shook her head.

'It's beautiful there, strange though,' he said. He lit a cigarette. 'But the goddam strangest place I ever saw you won't have heard of. Weird.'

'What is it?'

'The Rock...'

'The Rock?'

'That's it. It's why I'm here.' He pointed at the floor. 'We were carrying supplies for the guys there.' He coughed and said, 'Hell, but I was sorry to see it like that.'

'Like?'

Dan thought. Orders forbidding talk about the Rock had been issued to all sailors visiting Mauritius, but he didn't care. 'It's an island... goddam crazy.' He wiped his brow and took a shot of rum. It went to his head. 'I saw it first at night and I thought "A space of darkness". The words just came to me, like the place was glowing with lights all night but they didn't make it light.' He dropped his cigarette and trod it out. 'You know what I mean?'

Odette shook her head. Dan widened his eyes. The look scared her. She wished he'd leave her. Nothing he said made sense. He took another drink and offered her the bottle. She shook her head.

He said, 'Most of it's jungle, but they've built a fence where the sites stop; keeps people like me away from the rest of the island. The rest's like they're building another Subic. Hundreds of goddam Seabees stoned out of their minds. The lagoon's full of trash.' He unbuttoned a shirt button. 'And nowhere. It's nowhere. Thousands of miles in any direction...' he spread his arms, 'there's just nothing. Okay. So it's a B52 from the Mid-East, okay! So what?'

He talked about weapons dumps and nuclear submarines riding in anchored pairs as bombers and reconnaissance aeroplanes taxied along the aprons that surrounded the new runways. 'Still,' he said, 'they built a television station there. It had its moments... but nowhere. Diego Garcia they...'

'Diego...' Odette stuttered, and put a hand to her face.

'Honey?' Dan put his bottle on the floor and put an arm around her shoulders. She stiffened. Tears were pouring down her face. 'What's the matter?' She shook her head.

'I don't want to hear,' she said.

'Hear what?'

She swallowed. 'Diego Garcia.'

'What do you know about it?'

'I...' she said, and couldn't finish.

'Okay,' said Dan. 'We'll party instead,' and he tipped her back on the bed.

19

'Get off the wall! Do something!'

'We've got food, haven't we?'

'Not enough.'

'Why not?'

'I couldn't get enough money!'

Leonard shrugged. 'You'll get it,' he said.

'But why's it always me?' Odette shouted. 'You never go!'

'It wouldn't make any difference if I did. You know that! What did I get last time? Ten cents?'

'Ten cents buys something. And it meant I didn't have to beg so much. Anything – you know, Leonard?'

He shrugged again. Sullen, bad-tempered boy. People were used to seeing him on the wall. When he wasn't there, people asked where he was. When he was there, they didn't notice him. The wall was made of large stones, was crumbling at one end and going nowhere.

'Leonard?'

'What?'

'Did you hear what I said?'

'Yes!'

(Yes. He had no idea where his sister went at night. Once, she'd decided to tell him where she got her rupees from, but didn't know how he'd react. He'd grown unpredictable.)

'Then why don't you do something? Anything...'

'Look!' He flared his nostrils and bent down to put his face next to hers. He breathed over her. He had foul breath. 'I am sitting here, doing no one any harm! No trouble! I can't do anything! If I beg I get nothing, I can't fish here, I can't work anywhere else.'

'You've never tried.'

'I have!' (This was true. Once, he'd been to the docks and watched the ships unloading. The sea was flat, stained with oil slicks and plastic bags. Men worked cranes and loaded trucks. Others filled warehouses with boxes and bales. I can do that, he thought, and asked a man in overalls. This person pointed to an office.

'Ask for Mr Rene.'

Mr Rene had no vacancies for Ilois. 'Maybe next summer,' he said, and showed Leonard the door.)

'So you went to the docks once! I go to town every day!' Odette spat. Other people, gathering around to listen to the argument, agreed with her. 'She does.'

'I'll go back in the summer. That's what he said, and he was important! Have you met any important people?'

(Odette wondered if she'd ever had an important man inside her. She played back voices she remembered.)

'No,' she said. 'I don't think I've met any important people.'

'There!' he said. Triumphant for a change. He lay back and gobbed at a passing dog.

'So! You've met someone like that. He's going to give you a job one day.'

'Yes.'

'And that means you don't have to beg?'

'Yes…'

'Then why don't you do some cooking?'

'I don't do cooking.'

'Why not?'

'Because I don't know how to…'

'I'll show you!'

'You won't!'

'Then light a fire!'

'No!'

Leonard and Odette had no proof that they had ever lived in the Chagos. They visited officials about the compensation, but these men shook their heads and said, 'Look! There're thousands of people claiming to be Ilois! If we give something to everyone who says they are, there'll be none left for people who deserve it.'

'We lived on Diego Garcia! Ask anyone!'

'Where're your birth certificates?'

'We lost them.'

'Where?'

'I think on Peros Banhos.'

'But you said you were from Diego Garcia? What were you doing on Peros Banhos?'

'Coming here...'

'Yes?'

'We...'

'NEXT!'

Odette vomited over the official floor. Leonard yelled at a policeman on the steps outside. He helped his sister home, propped her in the shack and told her he'd be back in the evening.

Since she'd told him she was pregnant and explained how, he'd been shaken out of his lethargy. As soon as he was needed he understood. 'I'll be back in two hours.' He held up two fingers.

He learnt to plead and hassle around the bus stations and outside the tourist offices and airline offices. He held people's eyes until they gave him something. He swore at them if they didn't. He clenched collected coins until his knuckles turned white – he held Odette's hand tight when she went into labour and screamed for hours before a boy was born, dropped onto the floor of the shack and suckled on an arrangement of sacks.

Odette called him Jimmie. The baby cried at night, and when Leonard looked at him and his sister's glazed expression he was forced into thinking that begging wasn't enough. 'I'm going to see Mr Rene again,' he said.

'You won't be long...'

'No. An hour. I'll tell next door to call in.'

Mr Rene gave him a job. He was put with a gang of Mauritians who took no account of his feelings. Leonard confirmed everything they'd heard about the Ilois. He had nothing to say, couldn't read newspapers, couldn't drive a car, never watched television. He knew nothing about anything except Diego Garcia, and, 'We can't go home'. Trying to explain, he said this to his work-mates many times, 'We can't go home.'

'Nor can I!' said one. 'My wife says "you put one foot inside that door and I'll call my brother!" He's a big man! I know what you mean! Don't talk to me about going home!'

Leonard shook his head. Mr Rene told him to shift twenty bales of cotton from the Customs House to the store.

'To what store?'

'That one!'

Heaving on ropes and pulling carts. Cutting his hands and hurting his back. Dock work was hard work, but he was paid and by the ocean. Oily, but still ocean; his workmates began to give him a break, one day he even came home singing.

'Don't waste it on yourself,' Odette said.

'What?'

'That song. Sing it to Jimmie.' She cradled the baby and rocked him. 'He likes music. Go on!'

Leonard sang a song he'd heard on a radio. Passing people stopped, listened and nodded in appreciation. The man had a good voice, the song was about love and sent the baby to sleep.

'You do that every evening,' she said, 'and one day we'll find somewhere better.'

'Sure we can.'

Song. On Diego Garcia, song was an important diversion. Fishermen sang rowing songs in rhythm to their oar-strokes. Mothers sang 'Segas zenfants' to instruct their children. Others sang love songs to the accompaniment of coconut shell lyres and banana leaf and rice shakers. Leonard sang 'Hey Jude', all the way through, and then again when people applauded and yelled 'MORE!'

20

Leonard sat on a wharf, ate bread and drank one bottle of beer. He had been working well, Mr Rene had said. Someone else told him about a shack on Tombeau Bay. A Jo had lived in it and watched for a hotel owner. Now he was dead, the place was empty and someone else would have it.

'Watchman?' said Leonard.

'Yes.'

'I could do that.'

'You and a few more...'

'Tombeau?'

'Yes. There'll be a queue.'

Leonard sent word to Odette and left work early. He walked to Tombeau Bay. It was three miles away and the traffic choked but his spirits rose as he took the road that skirted the bay. It was quiet. Banana and coconut palms shaded the beach... something like a vague life he remembered.

He followed directions he'd been given, and met a man called Albert. 'Hello.'

'Good evening...'

'Where's the queue?' he said.

'What queue?'

'They said there would be, for the job.'

'What job?'

'The watching.'

'You've come for it?'

'Yes.'

Albert was the owner. His hotel was a boarding house but clean, popular and heading towards a Tourist Board rating. He planned extensions and new furniture for the rooms. A swimming pool. He did some car hiring and wanted to expand that side of the business. The shack was on a patch of ground above the beach. Palms and causarias grew around, and there were broad views of Port Louis, the bay and the reef beyond.

The watchman had to keep a casual eye on passers-by. 'No rubbish in the hotel,' Albert said. 'It's night work mainly, rest of the time you do what you want. Jo fished.

'I fished, ' said Leonard. 'I fished.' He said it again, to himself. He liked the idea that he might again. He thought about his father and the things Paul had taught him on Peros Banhos…'I fished.'

'You've got a rod?'

'I'll make one. And I'll watch well too.'

'Will you?'

'Oh, yes.'

'Good.' Albert was a sympathetic man. Ilois people were becoming Mauritius's racial butt – Albert had an open mind.'Good,' he said again, and gave Leonard the job.

'How long for?'

'As long as you're good at it,' Albert said, 'it's yours.'

Leonard, Odette and Jimmie moved a week later. It didn't take them long. They didn't have much to carry. They had a few rupees and smiled all the way.

Watch work was easy. No one bothered Leonard. He spent his off-duty time fishing. The noise of the ocean along the shore, the feel of it over his feet any time he wanted, the sight of it disappearing into the distance. Emerald hedges and glossy leaves; he was reminded of home but not depressed by the reminding at that time.

Odette laughed and told him old stories. Away from the noise and smoke and traffic of Port Louis; when Jimmie was old enough to walk, Leonard decided to teach the boy to fish. He cut a whippy rod, tied it with twine, found a hook and gave it to him.

'Look Jimmie! Just like mine!'

They walked the shore. Odette watched. She smiled and lay back. She ran sand through her fingers and listened to birds chatter.

The shout of a child, the encouragement of an uncle, a helping hand, a paddle through pools and onto rocks to cast. Sea like visible heat, crabs scuttling across the beach, some fish spotted in the shallows.

'Over there!'

'Breakfast!'

Breakfast.

They were proud of their catch and the catches they made over following weeks. Nothing much, but it was fishing. Leonard wrapped one in a banana leaf and said, 'You carry that one,' to Jimmie.

'Mine,' the boy said to his mother.

'You're clever! Did you catch it yourself?'

'Yes!'

It was low season. The hotel was empty. Albert walked down to the beach with a radio and a bottle of rum, and when Odette offered him a plate he said, 'Why not?' and patted Jimmie's head.

'Mine!' the boy said, holding up his fish.

'Did you catch it?'

'Yes!'

Leonard was pleased to have his boss visit but Odette worried that she didn't have rich enough food. Albert smiled and licked his lips.

'Nothing like it,' he said. 'Cooking out doors,' and to give the meal more atmosphere he turned the radio on and they listened to Sega music as they ate.

When he'd finished, Jimmie danced across the beach to the sea. He called his mother.

'He wants you,' said Albert.

'He never wants anything else,' said Odette, but she didn't mind. She stood up, brushed sand off her palms and walked across the beach. 'Come here,' she said, and took Jimmie's hands and led him into the water and out again, swinging and lifting him up.

'You like the Sega?' Albert asked Leonard. He'd been watching his sister and wishing he had someone like she had Jimmie. 'Yes,' he said.

'I was a singer in a band once.'

'Were you?'

Albert nodded. He pointed across the bay. 'In Port Louis. We were the most popular. The best!' He clapped his hands and smiled at the thought. 'But now there's the hotel and the cars. I haven't got the time.' He lit a cigarette and passed the bottle. 'No time...'

Leonard didn't say anything. Time didn't mean the same to him as it did to his boss.

'But maybe,' said Albert, 'I'll make time later.' He dragged on his cigarette. 'When I'm older.'

He watched Odette dance. She placed her feet carefully, twisted her waist and spun away across the beach.

21

When Albert didn't need him and he wasn't fishing, Leonard was happy to sit on the beach and play with Jimmie, or just watch. Ships rode anchor in the bay, men in fishing boats shouted to each other. Men with rods cast from rocks, the ocean boiled over the reefs beyond with a roar of smashed coral and spindrift. Odette knelt in the door of their shack and sorted rice. A new scarf her brother had bought her kept her hair tidy.

'You didn't steal it?'

'No! Look! I've got the price.' He waved a receipt. 'See?'

She smiled. 'Thank you.'

Albert came from the hotel. He was wearing shorts and new running shoes. 'Leonard?'

'Yes!'

'Leonard! We've got a delivery.'

'Delivery?'

Some of the rooms were being equipped with new beds. 'Beds,' said Albert.

'How many?'

'Ten.'

'Ten!'

'And they won't move without us. Come on.'

'Coming.'

Leonard had never seen ten beds grouped together outdoors. The delivery man had lined them up on the pavement outside the hotel. They had been made in a Mauritian workshop... 'Show me a better bed and I'll show you a square rupee,' said Albert.

'There isn't a square rupee,' said Leonard.

'Pick up that end,' said Albert, 'and mind the corners on the paint.'

The two men carried the first bed to room twelve. They put it opposite a window.

Leonard had never seen inside any of the rooms. He admired the wallpaper, the bedside table, the cupboard with a mirror, the glass in the window and the light bulb with a yellow shade. A coil of mosquito repellant, a tiny shower room.

'Very neat,' he said.

'Come on, nine to go.'

Leonard liked the next room the most. It was on the hotel roof, set aside from the others. Easy chairs and recliners were scattered across the roof; the hotel wasn't full, but one or two tourists were relaxing, chatting and dabbing lotions on their bodies. Some of these people were young and held hands. Gorgeous women lay beside thickening men with moustaches and small feet. The women wore the kind of swimsuits that blind voyeurs, the men wore expressions that made Albert wonder how their women could be so blind.

Leonard stared at them. Albert said, 'Don't stare, come on,' and led the way with the bed. 'In here.'

The roof-top room was luxurious. Light from four windows filled it, a personal bath in a separate room was there. A telephone and a colour television set were also provided. The floor was covered in a deep carpet. This was cream-coloured; Leonard had never walked on anything like it.

'Nice,' he said.

'Not bad,' said Albert. 'The best in the place,' he added, and stroked the television set.

'How much?'

'Ha!' Albert laughed and put his hand on Leonard's shoulder. 'How much?' He shook his head. 'Come on…'

When the two men got back to the street, children were walking down the road. School had finished for the day, boys swung their satchels at each other, girls held hands and talked about boys. Rude boys and ones on mopeds.

'This one's for number four,' said Albert.

'Four,' said Leonard.

'Excuse me?' said a tourist.

'Can I help?' said Albert.

'Yes. I want to hire a car.'

'Certainly sir. Wait there, Leonard; I'll be back in a minute. This way…'

'Thank you,' said the tourist.

Leonard sat on one of the beds and waved to some children. They laughed at him.

'What sort of car would you like?' said Albert. 'A Renault?'

'That'd be okay.'

'Or a Leyland? We have both.'

'No. A Renault would be fine.'

'A Renault 5?'

'Fine.'

'Or a Renault 12?'

'No; the 5 would be fine.'

'Are you sure?'

'Yes.'

'Then please sign here.'

The tourist wanted to visit Pamplemousses Gardens. He had heard about them, and traced the route with a finger on a map he spread on a table. Albert fetched the car, Leonard watched a man drive a cow down the road. 'Hello!' he shouted. The man didn't answer. He was deaf, and his only interest was his cow.

When the tourist had driven away, Albert came back and said, 'It's number four for that one, isn't it?'

Leonard shrugged. 'I think so.'

'So do I.'

Number four was one of the cheaper rooms. It shared a shower with rooms three, five and eight, and its window had a view of a wall.

'In here… mind the paint!'

'I am.'

'Move that table.'

'This one?'

'Yes!'

Other beds went to other rooms; when there was only one left and they went to collect it from the pavement, they found a schoolboy lying on it.

'Hey! Get off!' Albert yelled. 'That's new!'

'Yes,' said Leonard. 'The boss doesn't want his stuff dirty. Up! Move!'

The boy sat up. He was tired. Every morning he had to milk five goats before he left for school. When he got home he had to milk them again, clean their shed and do any other work his mother wanted him to do. 'I was tired.'

'Haven't you got a bed at home?'

'Yes…'

'Then use it! Come on…'

The boy swung his legs off the bed and stood up. 'I'm going,' he said, and as he walked away, Leonard and Albert carried the bed into the hotel.

When they finished and washed their hands, the two men sat on the veranda and drank beer. A couple in love came down from the roof, spread their towels on the beach and waded into the sea. Albert watched Leonard watch them. He lit a cigarette. 'Nice-looking girl,' he said.

Leonard didn't say anything. He'd been thinking about cars. Since he'd been in Mauritius, he'd seen many different types of cars. He wanted one with clean black tyres. Albert nudged him and said, 'Beautiful…'

Leonard blinked. 'What?' he said.

'Her!' He pointed.

Leonard shrugged.

'Have you got a girl?' Albert knew he hadn't. He drank some beer and leant back. He was curious. 'Eh?'

Leonard shook his head. 'No,' he said. 'Not really.'

'What do you mean? Not really?'

'I haven't.'

Albert lit two cigarettes and passed him one. 'Maybe you should. I could fix you up.'

Leonard shook his head, stood up, walked across the veranda and down to the shack. Albert could go to hell with questions. He took his fishing rod and set off along the beach, past the swimming guests and cast a line into a pool beyond a stack of rocks.

It is easy to kill a fish. They drown in air or with more kindness you can bash their heads out on rocks with a stone. Fish ooze and don't appear to show grief or pain, but once dead they still move. Leonard felt one squirm in his pocket. He took it out and stuck a knife in its eye.

He worked absentmindedly, letting his mind skip over thoughts and memories as he watched the end of his line and another fisherman working his way towards him. 'Anything?' the man yelled.

'This.' Leonard took the fish out of his pocket and held it up. It had stiffened into the shape of a crescent moon. 'You?'

The other man shook his head. 'Nothing!' He laughed. He didn't mind. He was a builder and only had the rod for fun and to keep away from home. His wife had six children. One was far thinner than the others. He was a fat man, his wife was a fat woman. He imagined her fancying a lean postman but he wouldn't say anything. His fat was waste, hers was muscle. She had red eyes and didn't mind him fishing. 'Never mind...' he said.

Leonard didn't agree. He wanted to be serious about fishing. One day, he thought, I'll have one of those, as he watched the boats along the shore. Some were old and others had fresh paint. He remembered everything he had learnt on Peros Banhos, and when the man passed him and said, 'Goodbye,' he didn't say anything.

22

Leonard sat below the hotel veranda and watched for suspicious characters as the noise of a disco at the best hotel on Tombeau Bay floated in the air. It annoyed Albert. He came out and swore. He couldn't afford the lights and the hi-fi system. One day he would. Now he was thinking about a swimming pool. The watchman's shack would have to go.

He said, 'Okay?' to Leonard and went back to the bar. He had some interesting guests from England. They drank whisky and were very informative. They had visited America and Australia and knew a lot about mining. They were in Mauritius to meet a man about bauxite, and were full of ideas.

Odette came and sat with her brother. She noticed different things. She ignored the noise of the disco and listened to the sea as it broke along the shore. She sniffed the air. The smell of burning rubber, salt, Leonard. She leant back, closed her eyes and sighed.

'We're lucky,' she said.

'Lucky?'

'Yes.' She opened her eyes and pointed. 'Look...'

'At what?'

'At what we've got!' She raised her voice.

Leonard laughed. He didn't see anything. If she'd pointed at something different or something they owned – she didn't. She was satisfied with forgiving the people who had forced them there and saying, 'There're people who'd give anything for this. You know some of them too.'

'I don't!'

'You do and know you do. In Roche Bois, remember?' She looked into his eyes. 'You're a liar.'

'Don't call me that...'

'Why not?'

'Because I'm not!'

Odette laughed.

'Haven't you got anything to do?' Leonard raised his voice. 'I'm working.'

'You call this work?'

'Yes! Where'd you think we'd be without it? We wouldn't have the beach and you wouldn't be able to come up here and point at what you think we've got.'

'Leonard…' She put her hand on his and shook her head. 'I'm sorry.'

He grunted, stood up and walked around the veranda, turned the corner, waved to the kitchen staff and checked around the front. Nothing was happening. The road was quiet. The noise of the last record being played at the disco drifted down. He imagined the dancers and walked back to the beach.

The dawn sky was the colour of a mullet's nose. Two men walked along the beach carrying plastic bags.

'That's the place,' said one.

'You sure?' said the other.

The first nodded. 'The third from those trees. I wrote it down. Look!' He had a piece of paper.

'You're right. Well done!'

'Ssh…'

The place was the hotel. The two men hid themselves in the shadows of a banana tree and talked about the watchman. 'No problem,' said the first. 'He's only an Ilois. He'll be asleep.'

The second man laughed. 'Good old Ilois,' he said.

'Yeah.'

Leonard snored. He'd stayed up to watch until three o'clock and then gone to bed. Jimmie had a restless night but didn't bother him. The two men crept past the shack, climbed the steps to the hotel veranda and inspected a window.

All the windows were barred with screens of scrolled iron. They tried a door. It was locked. They looked up at the guests' rooms. Some of these had open windows, but were out of reach. 'Come on. We'll check the kitchen. This way.'

A kitchen window was open.

'Beautiful!'

The two men climbed up and into the hotel. They trod carefully, past the cookers, sinks and piles of vegetable peelings to the dining room. They took shallow breaths and cocked their ears. The noise of the sea on the reefs and shore, the sound of a bedspring twanging. A gurgle through the water pipes, a mosquito whining through the reception area. Tables and chairs. A clock ticked. 'Over there,' whispered one of the men, and he pointed.

'Where?'

'There!'

'Beautiful…'

Rows of bottles stood on mirrored shelves. Rum, whisky, brandy, gin, wine, beer. 'See?'

The men filled their bags with bottles. 'Let's take the cigarettes.'

"Course we'll take them. Idiot.'

'Idiot? Me?'

'Yeah.'

'Look!'

'Ssh…'

The bottles chinked together. The men held the bags close to their bodies. Something surprising in a dream shook Leonard awake. 'Where?' he said, sat up and remembered.

The colour of the light was changing in subtle and washy ways. Leonard heard a noise. Footsteps, voices, chinking. He looked across the shack. Odette was asleep. Sometimes she talked in her sleep but never with a man's voice. 'Ssh,' he heard, and, 'careful. There's a fence there.'

'Where?'

'Watch it!'

115

Watch what? He wondered, stood up and put his head outside. The men were crossing the grass below the shack, about to hop the fence that bordered the beach.

'Hey!' he yelled, and ran towards them. 'What are you doing?' Odette woke up.

'Look who's here!' said one of the men.

'Oh, beautiful…'

'STOP!' Leonard reached the men. A fist hit him in the mouth. Lights exploded in his eyes, he fell over, a foot took him in the side and another in the head. 'Bloody Ilois,' he heard, and, 'Bastard. You didn't have to wake up.'

'HEY!' Odette yelled. She ran from the shack. She was naked. The two men looked at each other. Leonard groaned. He tried to stand up but another foot kicked him. A trickle of blood dribbled over his chin. One of his teeth fell out and lay in the sand.

'HEY!' Odette picked up a piece of driftwood. Bent nails stuck out of it. She spaced her legs apart and waved it over her head. The men licked their lips. They didn't know what to do. Odette yelled, 'ALBERT! QUICKLY!'

Albert didn't come. Leonard groaned. One of the men said, 'Where is he then?' and moved towards her. He put his bag down. The other man did the same. They looked at each other and back at her.

'What are you going to do?' one said.

'Yeah,' said the other, 'before we do something to you!'

'Shall we?'

'Why not? I haven't had a piece for days.'

'ALBERT!' She waved the driftwood. Her breasts had big nipples, 'ALBERT!'

'Albert?' said one of the men. 'You know I don't think he's coming. He's probably tucked up nice and warm, like you should be.' He winked. 'Eh?'

'ALBERT!' Leonard tried to move, 'QUICKLY!'

A hotel light came on, a door slammed, the men blinked, looked back at each other and ran off.

At breakfast, Albert was sorry about Leonard's injuries but not enough not to shout. He banged a fist on the table and narrowed his eyes. He had a headache.

'You're the watchman! It's your job! That's hundreds of rupees' worth they stole.'

Odette stuck up for her brother. 'He did the best he could. We both did. What do you expect?'

'Better. Nothing like this happened when Jo was here. Twelve years he worked for me – nothing.'

'I'm sorry,' said Leonard. 'It won't happen again.'

'You bet...'

Jimmie wriggled out of Odette's arms and chased a dog down the beach.

'Because if it does it'll be the last time. Understand?'

Leonard understood.

'Good.' Albert was calm now, but gave his voice an edge. 'Good.'

Leonard nodded and Odette took his hand. He felt bad, and later, when she said she'd cook a favourite food, he just shrugged and she saw in his face an old bloody look. The look from walls he'd sat on, and life in Tombeau, Cassis, Roche Bois, Peros Banhos and Diego Garcia, in that order.

23

Leonard dreamt about smashed bottles and saw a blue Albert shouting, 'That's it! Off! Stupid Ilois...' Suns bled, dead fish floated through the sky and bumped into him.

Cannons flashed. The girlfriend he didn't have appeared stripped. Birds and butterflies drank her sweat as she rolled around in a cool, grassy place. Her eyes sang and his dueted with them. Both pairs were clear and saw way into a future that whispered a list of all the brilliant things that were going to happen to them. They would travel overseas in a huge white ship and visit places from pictures they had both seen and fancied. Europe and America, Australia, Japan and the South Sea Islands. She would wear a new dress every day. He would carry a suitcase of clean shorts and shoes. Jimmie cried and woke him up.

His pride in having a watchman's job slipped. His natural sullenness took on a paranoiac dimension. He imagined Albert was watching him all the time. He imagined laughing girls and thieves in banana trees and hedges; when he was off duty he walked as far from the hotel as he could and fished on his own.

'Take Jimmie!'

'I'll catch more on my own.'

Odette laughed. 'You? Catch more?'

'I will!'

He didn't. He came back, mumbled and sat on the beach. He put his rod down and gave it a hard look.

'Nothing,' he said, and spat. His cheeks were pinched and he punched a fist into the palm of his other hand. 'Nothing,' and he watched the spit dry.

Fishing brought back memories of the Chagos and Paul on a dead flat lagoon with two lines. Tombeau wasn't home. A dead day and a waste of time. He didn't want anything to eat, didn't want to be bothered and didn't say anything else. His face cracked and his mind collapsed into a hole behind his eyes. He scooped a handful of dirt.

'Odette!'

'Yes?'

'Is Leonard back?'

'Yes.'

Albert came down from the hotel. He was carrying a chair. He put it outside the shack.

'Would you like this?' he said.

'What?'

'The chair. No charge.'

Odette looked at it. 'A present?'

'If you like.' Albert turned to Leonard. 'Leonard?'

'What?'

'Would you like it?'

Leonard shrugged. What did Albert mean? What did he want? He looked at his sister. Jimmie yelled and sat in the chair. Odette smiled.

She liked Albert. He had had words with Leonard but she understood why. He paid money to have the place watched. Leonard understood too, but in a different way. He understood with the aches he still felt from the beating. He had never expected to be hurt. He had never expected to live in Mauritius. His mind could only cope with certainties. He didn't want to say anything about the chair.

'Leonard? Albert's talking.' Odette stood up, picked Jimmie up and sat in the chair.

'I know.' Leonard picked his nose. 'Yes. Thanks.'

'It's old,' said Albert. 'The back's broken, but we've got some new ones and I thought…' He pointed to the shack.

'It's very comfortable,' said Odette, and touched his hand.

Odette liked Tombeau. It was safe for Jimmie. In Roche Bois or Cassis too many Ilois children were treated badly. Their lack

119

of sophistication was taken for stupidity. They were teased and taunted at school, blamed for things they hadn't done and left out of games.

Tombeau had children but Odette and Jimmie didn't mix. They had a patch of grass beside the shack, a skirt of beach below that, the rocks beyond and the shallows. Trees grew all around, the air smelt of water. Odette wanted to stay there.

She liked Albert. He had girlfriends – she knew she didn't stand a chance against them, but whenever he was about she watched herself and told Leonard to behave.

'Don't grumble. He gave you the job...'

'I know.'

'Tuck your shirt in.'

'It's torn at the back.'

'Give it to me and I'll mend it.'

'Then what'll I wear?'

Why did she nag? He went to the shop for a beer. Some people there whispered when he paid the money, and he felt them pointing as he left. He sat by the road to drink.

Albert liked Odette. She had a pride in something, a quality none of his girlfriends had. They'd complain if he tried to kiss before they'd taken their make-up off. 'IT'LL SMUDGE!' They didn't like their clothes crumpled, 'NO!' Odette's dress had holes in it.

'Get Leonard to buy you something new,' he said.

'He bought this.' She showed him the scarf.

'It's nice. Very nice. But what about a dress?'

'Oh,' she said. 'I'm not, sure. The money...' She stopped.

'What about the money?'

'He gives me some, for Jimmie and other things, but he keeps the rest.'

'I'll tell him...'

'No!' Odette stood up. 'No.' She didn't want him to think she'd been talking behind his back. 'I'm alright. I don't want anything but what I've got; apart from...' She sat down again.

'Apart from what?'

'Nothing.'

Albert wouldn't argue. Later in the day, he took a car to Port Louis and visited an uncle's shop.

On Diego Garcia, women had worn colourful clothes. Dresses and skirts printed with giant flowers were favourites, a matching scarf tied in a particular way. Albert said, 'I want something bright,' to his uncle. 'Something with flowers.'

'Which one's this for?'

'You don't know her.'

'No?'

'No,' said Albert. 'She's an Ilois I…'

'An Ilois?' The uncle laughed. 'Your watchman's woman?'

'She's his sister.'

'Oh, yes?' The uncle looked at his nephew.

'It's not like that.'

'No.' The uncle looked through his rails. 'Of course not.' He sucked his teeth. 'How about this?'

He showed Albert a white dress printed with big red flowers and green leaves. He put it on the counter and smoothed it. 'Special price for you.'

'How much?'

'Well…'

Albert gave his uncle a look. He had something on him. He'd seen him kiss a woman other than his aunt (his father's sister) in the back room of the shop. He got the dress cheap. His uncle wrapped it. 'Thanks,' he said, and drove back to Tombeau.

'There's no scarf with it,' he said when he handed Odette the parcel. 'But it's new.'

She unwrapped the dress and held it up. A breeze caught it and blew it against her body. 'Albert!'

'Put it on.'

'Now?'

'Why not?'

She was embarrassed. 'Well. I don't…'

'For me?'

It was the right size. She rubbed a sleeve against her cheek, smelt the material and ran her fingers over the flowers and leaves. 'It's mine?'

'Yes. Another present; but don't think you'll get another...'

Odette laughed. She kissed Albert on the cheek. Jimmie held his mother's leg.

Half an hour later, Leonard came back from doing nothing with his rod and sat down without a word. Odette said, 'Like it?'

He shrugged. He knew Albert had bought it. He could show off with money if he wanted. It was nothing to do with him. There were a hundred things you could do with your life. One of them was nothing. Why should he do anything when he couldn't catch a fish or watch a hotel properly? What did people expect?

'I love it.'

24

Leonard had left to go fishing and was late home. He should have been back by six o'clock. 'Never later,' Albert had told him. It was ten.

Odette went to the hotel and asked for Albert. 'He's not back,' she told him. 'It's not like him.'

'No?' He locked the bar and pocketed the keys. 'Then we should look for him. He might've hurt himself.'

'He wouldn't like that...'

'Wouldn't like what?'

'Us out looking.'

'Odette?' Albert took her chin in his hands. 'He wouldn't like it if he was lost and we didn't look for him! He might be praying for us to come along.'

Odette thought about that. 'He'll find somewhere to sleep,' she said. She didn't feel he was hanging off some rocks. 'Besides, we wouldn't see him anyway.' The sky was black. 'I'll just wait here.'

Albert shrugged. 'Okay. But if he's not back by the morning we'll go. Alright?'

Odette nodded.

'And don't worry about the watch. I'll sleep on the veranda.'

Odette walked back to the beach and sat down. It was dark, a fire was dying; embers blew in a warm breeze. Birds and geckoes rustled through the trees that hung their branches over the sand.

She creased her forehead, rubbed it and narrowed her eyes, picked up a stone and tossed it into the sea. Water shot into the air, the shivering lights of Port Louis blurred across the bay. A bird called, a stand of palm trees moaned. A restless goat shuffled, stood up, poked its nose at a bush and sat down again. The ocean slid up the beach, grabbed a ribbon of sand and dragged it back.

She stood up, rubbed the back of her neck, took a deep breath and walked to a string of rocks that stretched into the bay. She picked her way over them, stood on one and looked in every direction. She listened. No footsteps padded towards her. The sea splashed over her feet. A dog barked and a moped buzzed along the road that ran around the bay.

The night was humid. Her skirt stuck to the backs of her legs and she licked a line of perspiration off her top lip. He'll find somewhere, she thought but still whispered 'Leonard?' She missed him then, and wanted him to rely on her.

Jimmie cried. Odette stood up, walked to the hut, bent over him and straightened his blanket. She stroked his cheek and kissed him. He twitched his nose, flayed an arm and mumbled something about a tyre he'd found on the beach.

'Dirty... old car, now... won't wash.' He opened his eyes but was still asleep; he closed them, turned over and settled down.

'Jimmie...' Odette said. The boy made puckering noises. A rat ran through the shack. 'Sleep.'

She went back outside, sat on the beach again, tossed another stone and stared at the stars. She counted ten, gave up, rubbed her palms together, watched the Port Louis lighthouse blink and whispered, 'Where are you?' again.

'Is he back?' said Albert. The morning was hot and bright. Two mynah birds scrapped over a fish head. Jimmie yelled 'ALBERT!' and fell over.

'No,' said Odette.

'Come on then. You've eaten?'

'Yes.'

'And the boy?'

'He's okay.'

'Let's go.'

They picked their way along the beach. He smoked a cigarette and walked two steps behind her and watched her arches rise and the way she held her head. The dress he had given her flapped around her. Jimmie ran in and out of the sea. They headed towards the river estuary and asked people they met if they'd seen a man with a rod and a face as thin as the rod.

'No,' a postman said.

'He had a rod.'

'Many people with rods along here,' the man said. 'I could count hundreds every day.'

'You'd remember Leonard…'

'Would I?'

'Yes,' and Odette described him again.

'Is he bald?'

'No.'

The postman shook his head. He had a lot of mail to deliver, and the day wasn't getting any cooler. He wore a smart uniform but it was hot to work in, and he couldn't wait to see the last letter box. This was a mile away, so he said, 'No,' again and walked on. 'But if I see him, I'll tell him you're looking.'

'Thank you,' said Odette.

They walked as far as the point where the ocean became estuary, before turning to walk the inland road. They skirted the woods that ran down to the river, looked around and shouted.

'LEONARD!'

Women were washing clothes on stones, goats nipped bushes and trees. Odette asked if anyone had seen her brother. They shook their heads. 'No.'

'He's about this tall.'

'No.'

Jimmie got tired. He sat on a stone at the corner of a sugar-cane field and Albert took three bananas from his pocket. One for each. He joined the boy and lay back.

'If you don't wear boots in a sugar-cane field you'll go home bleeding,' he said.

'What?' said Odette. She didn't sit down. She shaded her eyes and looked around.

'My mother used to say that.'

'Why?'

'Because it's true, I suppose.' He pointed at the field. 'The first thing I remember is being on her back at harvest time,' he said. 'It was hard work.'

'Was it?' Odette threw her banana skin away.

'Yes…'

Odette turned to Jimmie. 'Finished?' she said.

He nodded.

'Already?' said Albert.

'He'll be waiting for us…'

'Where?'

'Wherever we find him. Come on.'

They headed towards Arsenal. People stood outside their houses and watched them pass. A queue at a bus stop didn't bother. Chickens ran across the road. Clouds of dust blew all around as an ox pulled a cartload of building rubble across a field. Albert said, 'I didn't think he liked it inland.'

'He doesn't. But he likes beer.' Odette pointed at a crowd of men outside a shop, leaning against a wall with bottles in their hands. 'I'll ask…'

'Thin man?' they said.

'Yes!'

'From Tombeau?'

'Yes.'

'He's called Leonard,' one of the men said. 'He slept here last night.' He pointed inside the shop. 'He left his rod.'

'What?' Odette didn't believe it. Leonard never went anywhere without his rod. 'He wouldn't.'

'He did. There.' The man pointed again.

The rod was leaning against a wall. Its master had gone and it was too far from the ocean.

'Oh,' said Odette, and picked it up. 'Where is he? He wouldn't just leave it.'

'That way.' The man pointed back towards Tombeau.

'But we just came that way. We didn't see him.'

'Maybe he's sleeping somewhere. He had a few this morning.'

'A few? This morning?' Odette shouted. 'He didn't have enough money for a few! And he shouldn't drink in the morning! He can't take it.'

The man laughed. 'We bought him some. He was sad.' He lit a cigarette. 'He's Ilois. They're...'

'I know who Ilois are!'

The man didn't say anything else.

Odette, Jimmie and Albert left the shop and walked out of Arsenal, past graffiti that read, 'Gunners are the greatest!' and, 'FA Cup for Gunners and all our friends'.

Albert carried the rod and thought it throbbed. Unfamiliar hands disturbed it. Soft hands. He felt awkward but gave it to Odette and held Jimmie's hand instead. It was late afternoon when they got back to the shack.

Leonard wasn't there. The place was as they'd left it. A dog was nosing around the fire. 'Shoo!' Jimmie shouted and chased it away while Odette sat down and Albert rested the rod against a tree.

'Maybe the man was right,' he said. 'He's probably sleeping the drink off.'

'No.' Odette wasn't convinced. She tuned the gift her mother had given her and imagined him confused and frightened, wandering through sugar-cane fields, chased by angry landlords and their dogs.

'I'll look again later.'

'No. You've got the hotel. There's your guests.' She pointed to some.

'They can look after themselves.'

'But...'

'No! I'll come!' Albert was firm. Leonard might have let him down once, and he'd been angry for a good reason but he liked the man, the woman more. 'Later. I'll meet you here.'

25

That evening, a policeman visited the hotel. He asked to speak to Odette.

'Why?' said Albert.

'I'll speak to her first.'

'She'll be on the beach.'

The day before, Leonard had left the shack and walked along the shore. He carried his rod like a flower, and cast from rocks. Black rocks, white sand and a clear warm sea. But the pools were empty, he didn't catch anything all morning, and lay down to rest when the sun got too hot.

When he closed his eyes, Diego Garcia's jungles whispered to him across the ocean. They talked about how no one cared for them any more. They were neglected and the ducks and chickens Ilois had been forced to leave behind roamed the undergrowth, wild and anxious. The sun was hot; Leonard shook himself awake and stood up.

He walked as far as the estuary, the limit of his fishing area. He stood on the furthest rock and balanced for an hour, casting and re-casting, dropping the line and waiting for a bite.

No bite. He chose another rock, and fished until the sun began to sink. A breeze blew off the ocean. The sky turned pink and he began to feel hungry. He thought he smelt Odette's cooking. He shook his head. She was a mile away. He reeled in and decided to go for a beer. Arsenal village wasn't far, and he knew people there.

He walked along the beach, thinking about nothing, and was about to climb onto the road when he noticed a blue boat, open-decked, sail furled, bobbing at its mooring. It was a beautiful sight and took him back again. When he half-closed his eyes it was Paul's from Peros Banhos in calm weather, waiting in the lagoon for a day's work. Real work, real fishing – Leonard needed a beer, shook his head and climbed up to the road.

He had enough money for one bottle. He drank slowly, watching men talk and women sit, and was about to leave the shop when someone said, 'Hey! You going?'

'Yes.'

'Why?'

'I...' Leonard put his hand in his pocket and jangled nothing. He shrugged.

'Come here,' the man said, and put his arm around Leonard's shoulder. 'I'll buy you one.'

Other people bought him more beer, and someone cooked him a meal when he said he hadn't eaten all day. 'You must eat,' they said. 'You'll waste away!'

Leonard wanted to tell them he'd wasted away already but didn't know how to explain himself. He was overwhelmed, his tongue glued to the roof of his mouth and the drink gave his sadness a frozen crust. He just nodded, whispered, 'Thank you,' and accepted another.

The shopkeeper offered Leonard a blanket and a bed. In his sleep he had a dream. (In it he found himself flying home. Maude and Raphael were waiting for him, Odette wanted to play in the lagoon. Friends brought him presents.

A radio, a basket of bananas, bottles of wine and rum, a new set of hooks.

'You deserve them,' they said.

He was surprised. 'Why?'

'The man's a hero and he says, "Why?" Leonard! You're too modest! Why!'

A feast was prepared, laid and eaten, toasts were drunk and the tropical day turned into tropical night. The stars came out and Leonard was fêted.

Massive lobsters were boiled in massive pots; rice was boiled and laced with rum. Musicians arrived, tuned their instruments and played traditional songs. People with masks and hats sang and danced in circles and chains; girls and boys disappeared into the jungle.

A woman came to him and asked a question. The noise of the party prevented him from hearing what she said, but his answer was the right one, so she took his hand and led him to a hut. She was very beautiful, and willing, and was about to show him something when a foot stepped out of the sky and ended the dream. The foot was clean and tattooed with the word 'WELCOME'.)

Leonard woke up with sweat streaming down his face and the blanket in a heap on the other side of the shack. The night was flushed with dawn and the first song birds began to chatter.

'Welcome,' he whispered. 'Where?' He wanted to go home. He sat in the doorway and watched the empty road.

Two hours later, he drank a glass of water and the shopkeeper offered him a banana.

'No thank you…'

'You must. It's good for you!'

'I don't want it.'

'Look! You have to eat something. You need food. You'll feel better.'

Leonard wouldn't argue. He ate, and the man was right. He did feel better and when he was offered a beer he didn't say, 'No'. Why not? he thought, and drank it all. He didn't care any more.

It was strong beer, and made him feel stronger.

'Better?' said the shopkeeper, and drank one himself.

'Yes. Thank you.' Leonard smiled. The first smile to crack his face in months. 'Thank you!' he said again, and he set off down the road, and headed for the shore.

Beer in the morning fuzzed him but gave him purpose. It swept away reason too, and gave everything a glow. Something he'd not noticed before, and a shine.

This bounced off the trees and covered the beach. He walked along it and looked across the bay. The blue boat was still there. In daylight it was even more remarkable to see. It was painted the same shade as Paul's had been and the rig was familiar. A simple thing to sail. The beer tipped him over the edge and he walked into the sea towards it, and then swam when it got too deep.

The water was warm and as calm as settled dust. He reached the boat, hauled himself over the gunwale, sat down and put one hand on the tiller, the other on the sail.

He only wanted to sit in it; to feel the boards holding him, listen to the rig creaking and smell the varnish and paint, but when he rubbed the sail and tapped the deck his mind flipped gears and he thought, Home. He moved the rudder and heard the ocean sing. 'I,' he said aloud, 'am Leonard...' He coughed. He felt beer force words. '... and going home now.'

So he cast the mooring rope, hauled the sail, trimmed the rigging and smiled as the boat's owner came running down the beach, shouting and waving.

'Hey! Thief! Come back!'

Leonard shook his head. He wouldn't listen.

'STOP THIEF! THIEF!'

Leonard wasn't a thief. No one could call him that. He pointed the boat to sea and the owner splashed into the water. 'COME BACK!'

No.

'HEY!'

It would take him a long time to reach Diego Garcia, but the sea was his brother. The currents were his friends and the wind would be kind all the way. He had a strong feeling that he had not made a mistake.

'STOP THIEF!'

Leonard didn't stop. He didn't look back. He didn't think about Odette or Jimmie or Albert or Tombeau Bay or anything to do with Mauritius as he steered the boat away. He tuned into his instincts and trimmed the sail. He watched the bow cut the ocean and felt the boards on the water. An old and powerful excitement filled him; he licked his lips and narrowed his eyes at the line of foam that broke over the distant reef.

As he sailed closer to this line, it roared. It warned and crashed before calming into the lagoon. Beyond the reef lay open sea and a deeper blue, higher waves and the Chagos Archipelago. 'Home,' he said aloud. He punched the air and steered towards a passage through the reef.

From the shore – even from fifty yards away – the waves breaking over the reef deceived by looking insignificant, but when the wind picked up out of nowhere and Leonard found himself having to trim the sail and control a suddenly bucking boat, any insignificance was gone.

The sea became a rage of foam and noise and shards of flying coral. He heaved on the tiller, wrapped two ropes around his hands and tried to turn the boat into the wind.

He swore. The passage he thought he'd seen turned out to be no passage at all, as he steered along the edge of the reef, steadying himself and the boat and shouting at the waves. He didn't want to bother them. He wondered why they wanted to hurt him. 'Don't!' he yelled, and turned the boat into their path.

He was soaked and licked his lips. They stung. The effect of the beer was wearing off, and he was beginning to doubt his wisdom. He turned to his rod for comfort. A friend that never let him down; he looked all over the boat and panicked when he couldn't find it.

He panicked as another wave smashed into the boat. He thought. He pulled on the tiller and wrapped ropes around his hand again. He remembered the beer shop in Arsenal, and saw his rod leaning against a wall there. He cursed as he forgot what he was doing and another wave picked the boat up and dumped it onto a shelf of fisted coral.

Wood splintered. The decks yelled and cracked, and the boat spun like a top. Wind filled the sail and pulled the rig sideways, towards the open sea and deep ocean.

'Wait!' Leonard yelled. 'My rod.'

The reef split the deck and wrenched the rudder off its hinges. Water spouted, and the boat bucked out of control. Leonard yelled 'Don't!' again, and his blood flushed with sweat.

'No!'

The boat filled with water. The rigging was ripped apart and the mast began to topple. Slowly at first, then quick and final, splintering in the air and falling into the sea as another wave picked the wreck and flung it across the reef.

The noise was deafening. Swords of wood and lengths of rope flayed around, the corals snarled and chided.

'What you doing here?' they said. 'There's no passage. We're the princes here.'

No passage. The wreck was lifted again, and tossed up with Leonard still clinging, to land, miraculously, on the other side of the reef.

The streak of foam and pounded coral was behind him, open ocean ahead, the deepest blue sky above, a few shattered planks of wood beneath. He looked at them, listened to the ocean, and stood on the remains of a deck seat before he sank, and the waves smoothed the spot where he had been.

He didn't care as he sank. Reason had filtered through beer, and told him he'd never reach the Chagos. It was too far, too rough, too deep. It told him to cut his losses and go home. But home wasn't home if it wasn't Diego Garcia, so he silenced reason and garbled, 'No!'

Under water it was warm and fuzzy, and the currents put their arms around his body and dragged him down. He joined fish and drifting weed, took water into his lungs, filled up and held his stomach, winced and closed his eyes, and saw his family and other people he'd known asking him what he thought he was doing. Georges carried a bottle of rum and put it to his mother's lips, or were they Odette's? His father smiled and the sun split open and leaked all over the sea.

His tongue flipped back and tried to find his throat. He swallowed and choked. He thrashed his arms and the currents laughed as they pulled, and pieces of the boat floated down around him like rain. Lumps of timber, hinges and metal runners.

He thought he heard a shout and an arm come to hold him. He tried to grab a piece of sinking mast before he felt a rush of warmth leave his body, and icy fingers feel their way over him. He opened his eyes for the last time before going limp and the currents let him go, so he could die alone, which is what he did in the sea beyond Tombeau reef.

'It didn't take us long to find him,' the policeman said. 'A crowd watched the whole thing from the beach. I'm surprised you didn't hear them.'

Odette shook her head. She'd been washing Leonard's other shirt as he had died.

'Where is he now?' said Albert.

'Port Louis.'

'Can I do anything?'

The policeman looked at him. He fingered his uniform and rubbed one of his buttons. He wasn't used to dealing with this sort of thing. 'You could stay with her.'

'Of course.'

'And there'll be some forms. She can't write.'

'I know.'

'If you could help with them I'd be...'

'Yes,' said Albert. He knelt beside Odette and took her hand. She was sobbing and held tight. He gave her a handkerchief.

The policeman opened his mouth. Words stuck in them, so he nodded and then he left.

26

Odette took Jimmie to bed, put her arms around him and squeezed. 'Jimmie...' She was scared. Albert stood in the doorway.

Calm night, soft water, the wreckage of the boat Leonard had stolen was washed up along the beach. Mynahs chattered. Jimmie sucked his thumb.

'You want me to stay?' Albert said.

Odette didn't say anything.

'I will,' he said. 'And I'll take care of things in Port Louis. Don't worry.'

'Thank you.' She wiped her eyes.

He shook his head. 'Anyone would do it,' he said.

She shook her head. She said, 'I met men who wouldn't.' It was late and she wanted to lie down.

She lay with Jimmie, Albert lay on an air-bed by the door. A slight moon cast soft light into the shack, spreading and outlining the Ilois's possessions. A saucepan. A mirror. A tea chest. A photograph of Queen Elizabeth the Second and the Duke of Edinburgh. A jar of rice and three eggs. Two bananas. A dead fishing rod.

She sniffed. She didn't sleep for an hour, but when she did she was restless. Jimmie made sucking noises. Albert stared at the moon before falling asleep. The sea breathed.

He woke up a few hours later. Everything was quiet. Nothing moved. He looked across at Odette. She'd flayed in sleep and the blanket had exposed her legs. They were smooth and shone in the moonlight. He stood up, walked over to her and covered them.

* * *

The policeman came back in the morning. He was carrying a black briefcase, and asked Albert to sign some forms. These were official, and sad to read.

'Where's he being buried?' said Albert.

'Port Louis. You'll be at the funeral?'

'Yes. But I wondered…' Albert hesitated.

'What?' said the policeman.

'There's a cemetery,' said Albert, 'at Souillac.'

'Yes.'

'A seamen's cemetery.'

'So?'

'Could we bury him there?'

'At Souillac? Why?'

Albert shrugged.

The policeman thought. It would involve re-organising, and more forms, but he said, 'Why not? If you can pay…'

'I can pay.' Albert showed him some money.

The policeman looked at the cash. 'I'll find out. You're M. Burnier?'

'That's right.'

'I'll come back later. You'll be here?'

'Yes.'

Leonard was buried according to Christian ritual, at Souillac. No spirit-seeker came and chased around with a switch. Nobody mentioned Minni-Minni. Jimmie said, 'Taxi?'

'Ssh and sit in the back.'

The grave was dug as close to the ocean as a grave could be. Albert paid the undertakers, the priest and the diggers. Odette thanked him, and promised to make it up.

They squinted as they stood at the grave. The smoke from a rubbish tip blew around and two children carried battered tin cans through the cemetery. Their clothes were torn and dirty, and they lived under seven sheets of galvanised iron. They watched the funeral party.

Odette, Jimmie, Albert, a priest, four pallbearers. The service was solemn as the wind blew and the sea roared all around them. It pounded into a frenzy on the shore. Souillac is Mauritius's southernmost village, and no reef protects that stretch of coast from waves born in the Antarctic. A strong wind blew clouds of sand into the sky and whirled them into the trees that bordered the cemetery. Sad words, a hymn and some verses from the Bible about fishermen waiting for storms to pass.

The cemetery stretched in every direction, the blocks of graves sectioned according to religion. Old vaults were open to the sky, their black blocks carted for a wall somewhere else. The tops of crosses were missing.

Leonard's coffin was lowered into the ground, and handfuls of sand were tossed. Sand and tears. The priest was kind and said that he was always available. He wanted to minister to his flock, and prove that Christ died so that men like Leonard could live. No one argued, and no one waited for the gravediggers to fill the hole.

27

Albert bought a table and put it in the hotel's reception. It was large enough to take a display of places to visit in Mauritius, a locked case of Sega cassettes and a spread of newspapers for guests to borrow.

He was pleased to be able to offer a better service. One day he would be able to afford flowers to arrange on the food and lamps on every dining-room table; he smacked his stomach, went to the veranda and chatted to some guests.

Smoking and accepting a drink from one of them, he looked down and across the beach to where the watchman's shack stood. A corner of its roof flapped in an unseasonal wind. He reminded himself to fetch some nails and a hammer to it.

When he'd drunk, he looked at his watch and said, 'I give myself an hour off now.' He picked up a newspaper.

'You deserve it,' the guests said, and, 'Friendly chap,' when he'd gone.

Odette liked him to read to her. She missed the sound of a man's voice and watched his lips move. He sat on the beach with her. 'What happened today?' she said.

Albert coughed and opened the paper. He looked at her and smiled before saying, 'There's been a fire in Mahebourg.' He ran his finger down the story. 'Three houses burnt down before they could put it out.'

'Oh...'

'But no one was hurt. A man down there's a hero now. He carried five children out through smoke-filled rooms!'

Odette watched the way Albert's hair fell across his forehead and waited for his hand to smooth it away from his eyes. She enjoyed the anticipation. He turned a page, tidied his hair and

she leant back. 'And there was an accident at Centre de Flacq.'
He shook his head. 'A bus hit a cow.'

Jimmie came back from fishing with a stick and string and
asked for some bread. He smiled and said, 'I nearly got one.'

Albert looked over the top of his paper and said, 'You won't
catch anything with bread…'

'I will!'

'If you say so.' Albert rummaged in his pocket for a packet
of cigarettes.

'Don't go far,' said Odette. 'And don't get lost.'

'I won't.'

Albert lit up.

Jimmie came back with a fish and laid it on a leaf. Albert said
he'd give them some potatoes but Odette said she had rice, so
he said he'd bring some wine down later, when the guests were
quieter and he didn't need to watch the reception.

In 1965, the British Government had delivered their terms for Mauritius's independence from the Empire. These terms hinged on the premise that Mauritius relinquish the Lesser Dependency of the Chagos Archipelago to the UK in exchange for £3 million. The archipelago and others besides would become known as BIOT – British Indian Ocean Territory – and the native population (the Ilois) would remain British subjects. A year later, Britain and the USA signed a deal stating that the island of Diego Garcia would 'become available for defence purposes for fifty years' and plans outlining the methods to be used in the uprooting, shipping, and dumping of 1,800 Ilois were presented in a file marked 'SECRET'. 'SECRET' was also the notice applied to the payments the US made to the British in exchange for the acquisition and depopulation of the islands: payments of $14 million in the form of written-off expenses incurred in the research and development of the Polaris submarine/missile system.

'The real impression of power came from the lagoon, and the gigantic assemblage of naval power and supplies. I could count seventeen ships riding at anchor. Thirteen were cargo vessels, stuffed to the gunwales with tanks and ammunition, fuel and water supplies, rockets and jeeps and armoured personnel carriers, and ready to sail at two hours' notice. There was an atomic submarine, the USS *Corpus Christi* – a batch of crewmen were even now sailing by in their liberty boat, off to see the delights of the Rock, and presumably, to ferret out some of the eighty women assigned to the base; there was the submarine tender USS *Proteus*, which I had last seen in Holy Loch, in Scotland, and which was packed with every last item, from a nut to a nuclear warhead, that a cruising submariner could ever need; and there was the strange white-painted former assault ship, the USS *Lasalle*, now converted into a floating headquarters for the US Central Command, and in the bowels of which admirals and generals played "Games of Survivable War in the Mid-East Theater", with the white paint keeping their electronic battle directors and intelligence decoders cool in the Indian Ocean sun.'

(In 1984, Simon Winchester visited Diego Garcia. The island is off-limits to unauthorised personnel, but in the few hours that he was allowed to anchor in the lagoon, this is what he saw.)

From Outposts, *published by Hodder and*
Stoughton, 1985

'Although we have no information, some deaths are no doubt bound to have occurred among the islanders in the normal course of events'

From a letter to Mr John Hastings from a Foreign Office official, 16 August 1976

This Book is Dedicated to Ilois Who Died as a Result of their Removal from the Chagos Archipelago, Including:

ELAINE AND MICHELE MOUZA: mother and child, committed suicide

LEONE RANGASAMY: born on Peros Banhos, drowned herself because she was prevented from going back

TARENNE CHIATOUX: committed suicide, no job, no roof

VOLFRIN FAMILY: DAISY VOLFRIN: no food for three days, obtained Rs 3 (about 20p) and no more as Public Assistance. Died through poverty

JOSUE AND MAUDE BAPTISTE: poverty – no roof, no food, committed suicide

Source: Comite Ilois Organisation Fraternelle

ACKNOWLEDGEMENTS

This book could not have been written without reference to the following organisations, authors and publications.

Francoise Botte. 'The Ilois Community and the Ilois Women' (University of Mauritius, unpublished thesis. 1980)

George Champion and the 1966 Society for Diego Garcians in Exile

Comite Ilois Organisation Fraternelle

Diego Garcia International Solidarity Committee (UK) 'Diego Garcia, 1975: the debate over the base and the Island's former inhabitants. Hearings before the Special Sub-committee on investigations of the Committee on International Relations, House of Representatives, 94th Congress' (US Government Printing Office, Washington, 1975)

The Joint Ilois Committee

John Madeley. *Diego Garcia: a contrast to the Falklands* (The Minority Rights Group, London, WC2N 5NT. 1982)

Robert Scott. *Limuria. The Lesser Dependencies of Mauritius* (Oxford University Press. 1961)

Herve Sylva. 'Report on the survey on the conditions of living of the Ilois community displaced from the Chagos Archipelago' (Unpublished report commissioned by the Minister of Social Security, Port Louis, Mauritius. 1981)

The Sunday Times

The Washington Post

The Guardian

Simon Winchester. Outposts – Journeys to the surviving relics of the British Empire (Hodder and Stoughton, 1985)

Special thanks to John Madeley, for his help and encouragement, and also to John Loader, for correcting me.

Made in the USA
Columbia, SC
25 August 2017